Hellish
Book One:
Tortured Souls

By Scott Dokey

Dedicated to my wonderful Mom, whom I know is looking down on me from Heaven. You are always in my thoughts

When darkness falls the shadow rises.

Humanity is what it despises.

The shadow calls upon fear to bring forth error.

Error brings forth the last ultimate terror.

From dust we began so shall we end.

Our flesh will be blood, with earth shall blend.

Valiant effort cannot dismay,

The finality of that day.

You cannot fight the inevitable.

And your life is always forgettable.

And when death's hand maintains a grasp.

And the voice is calling sharp and rasp.

From dust you began.

So shall you end...

—Michael Scott Williams

Chapter 1

The first one he beheaded was Gadreel.

Belial followed him down to the east bank of the Euphrates, where the current flowed swift and strong. The water was dark and dirty, filled with rotting plants and animals, the whole scene reeking of death and decay. It was a fitting place to find the answers he so desperately sought. If any of his brothers or sisters knew Lucifer's plan, it would be him.

"Gadreel!" he called out as he approached the water's edge. His armor was dented and splattered with blood, not his blood, though. He didn't know whose blood it was. It had dried on his breastplate, staining his armor like a gruesome celestial painting.

Dressed as a commoner, Gadreel's face was that of a man who had lost everything. His skin was pale and withered, as if his will to live had been sucked from him, causing him to shrivel up. He turned to face his brother, a tattered turban covering his head, shocked to hear his name called, and even more shocked to see Belial there. It didn't surprise him to see the angry look on his face, though, and he knew he had to tread carefully. "Belial! I'm surprised to see you. What can I do for you, Brother?"

"You can disperse with the pleasantries, Gadreel. I want answers, and I want them now."

Gadreel measured his words slowly, "I'm afraid I'm at a loss here, Belial. What answers are you looking for?"

Belial's eyes glowed bright red, and his nostrils flared like an angered bull. "Don't play games with me, Gadreel!"

Gadreel didn't know exactly what Belial was talking about, but he had a good guess. "I'm not sure what you believe to know, Brother, but something has clouded your judgment. You're not thinking straight."

"Don't you dare tell me how to think!"

"What I mean is simply that what happened, happened. There's no changing the past. It can't be undone."

"But I can make those that failed pay!"

"It's not a simple question of failure versus success. We fought long and hard, but in the end, we weren't strong enough."

"That's a lie! We should've crushed them. Our forces were more than enough to win."

"But they weren't, and we didn't."

Belial's smile grew like a crescent moon, and in the light of his eyes all that shone was madness. "It was you! You're the one who betrayed us! I should've known all along you'd be the one to sell us out to earn Father's good grace."

"That's not true, Belial. I was simply stating that we underestimated our opponent and overestimated ourselves. We all paid the price for our short-sightedness. Myself included."

"Liar!" Belial shouted. "You were against our plan from the beginning."

"And yet I fought with you. Why would I stand with you if I were against you? Listen to yourself, Belial. You're not making sense."

His words fell on deaf ears, as Belial's sword was already in his hands. The blood on the blade reeked of violence and stank of death.

Gadreel had one chance left to diffuse the situation. In a last-ditch effort, he turned his back on Belial and walked away. "I won't argue with you anymore, Brother. I've made my peace with Father's decision. I suggest you do the same."

He had hoped those last words would be enough to steel his brother's temper and give him the chance to flee. He should've known better. In Belial's ears, they were simply an arrangement of words, inconsequential sounds without meaning.

"How dare you turn your back on me, coward! Turn and face me!"

"I will not fight you, Belial."

"Then you will die like the traitor you are!"

Belial's blade hissed as it cut through the air, a diagonal slash that would've split Gadreel in two if he hadn't rolled out of the way at the last minute. While he was lucky enough to dodge the first attack, he wasn't fast enough to evade the second.

Belial recovered quickly and spun to his left as he brought his blade around. His eyes narrowed and his lips twisted into a sneer. His blade glinted in the flickering light, its edge sharp as razors as it raked across Gadreel's back, sending him crashing to the ground in agony.

Belial grabbed Gadreel's hair and yanked his head back. "I'm going to give you one last chance, Gadreel. Admit to your deceit and I may let you live."

Gadreel knew what was coming. He saw the look in

Belial's eyes; the blood-lust that had taken over. It wouldn't matter what he said at this point. Belial had already made his mind up. And if that was the case, he would die admitting his mistake and hope that his ultimate act of repentance would carry with him to the afterlife.

Gadreel summoned up his last ounce of strength, blood spraying from his mouth as he spoke, "The only thing I will admit to, Brother, is that I made the mistake of following you and Lucifer into battle, and I pray to our Father for his mercy and forgiveness."

Belial's eyes were raging infernos as he brought his sword around in a great arc, which bit through the flesh of Gadreel's neck and sliced his head off.

After Gadreel's body hit the ground with a wet thud, Belial reached down and picked up the severed head of his fallen brother, holding it in front of his face. The look of a man filled with remorse flashed over him for a quick moment as he realized what he had done.

Quickly, though, the eyes of a cold-blooded killer returned to reclaim their ocular residence. "Look what you made me do, Brother! It didn't have to come to this. All you had to do was tell me what I needed to know. But, no, you couldn't do that!"

He pulled his arm back and hurled the bloody head into the churning waters of the river. It splashed and sank, leaving a trail of crimson foam. The rest of the corpse he abandoned on the parched earth to rot and feed the swarming flies—a deserving fate for a coward.

Then he went in search of the others.

Uzziel was the next victim of Belial's wrath. He sat at the foot of the Great Pyramid, gazing at the starry sky with a heavy heart. Sand and dust carried the pungent scent of the ancient lands, of hidden secrets and distant fires, of life and death in endless cycles. He wished he could touch the bright lights that danced above him, and feel their warmth chase away his inner darkness. But before he could reach out, Belial appeared and ended his life in a brutal way, just like he did to his brother.

And after that, Arioch. His siblings had vanished to the edges of the earth, hiding from his fury. But Belial was unstoppable in his hunt, consumed by his need for the truth. He caught up with her after centuries of searching. She had tucked herself deep under the ground, in a bleak cave that no human could ever stumble upon. Belial was not human, though, and he faced her with his eyes ignited like hellfire. When she failed to satisfy his twisted logic, he ended her in a snap.

Haurus had fled to the open water, working as a deckhand on a merchant ship that navigated the Red Sea. He wished to forget the nightmares of the fall. Unfortunately, Belial found him waiting at the port in Elim, where the ship moored. Haurus cried for his life, trying to persuade Belial that he was not the traitor he accused. But Belial had grown deaf to the desperate pleadings of his people long ago. He snuffed him out swiftly.

There were many more after that, with each one ending as the first, leaving Belial more and more desperate for the truth. He was consumed by a burning thirst for answers that nothing could quench. He tried to wring out the secrets from his kin that he knew they were hiding, but they only gave him silence and defiance. He finally surrendered to the cruel reality that he would never know the answers he sought, no matter how much agony he unleashed on his brethren.

As he perched on the summit of the Andes, the highest and most majestic mountain range in the world, he gazed at the crimson snow that stained the pristine white landscape.

Another angel had fallen by his hand, another life snuffed out in his quest for the truth.

But then, a sudden revelation struck him like a bolt of lightning. He had been chasing shadows all along, blind to the real answer that lay before him! *It was Lucifer's fault! It had always been Lucifer's fault. He's the one I need to go after!*

And so, he got to work on a plan that would be both his revenge and salvation!

Chapter 2

Phlegethos had no stars to brighten its black sky, only the flickering light of fire that burst out of cracks in the rocky terrain. The air was filled with the roar of flames and the smell of sulfur. The earth shook constantly, as if a giant beast was stirring beneath the surface. Far away, molten lava poured down from jagged mountains, creating dazzling fire-falls that devoured everything in their path. This was a realm of fire and fear, where no one could escape the wrath of the inferno, and Belial was both its master and slave.

After a millennium of solitude, he still couldn't forget the bitter taste of defeat, the humiliation of losing a battle he should've won. The images of his enemies' triumph haunted his every waking moment, fueling his fury to a boiling point. He had abandoned his throne of Abriymoch and stormed out to find his allies, determined to make them pay for their failure and extract the truth from their broken bodies.

He had not realized the terrible price of his quest—the infernal bond that chained his soul to his hellish domain. As he wandered the world in search of answers, he felt his vitality draining away. His last fight in the Andes had pushed him to the brink of exhaustion, reducing him to a shadow of his former self. Then, in his darkest hour, he finally understood the truth. With a new resolve, he made his way back to Phlegethos, where he could recover and plot his next move.

The ashen road stretched out before Belial, a winding ribbon of gray that seemed to go on forever. The air was hot and dry, and the only sound was the crunch of Belial's footsteps on the ash.

Belial was deep in thought, lost in his own world, that he didn't notice the figure lurking in the shadows. The figure raised a dagger and hurled it at Belial, striking him in the chest with a loud thwack, causing him to stagger backward.

Belial looked down at the silver dagger protruding from his chest, and his eyes widened in pain. He turned to face his attacker, and saw the hatred in his daughter's eyes.

"Fierna," he said, "what are you doing?"

Fierna's eyes were cold and hard. "I'm doing what I have to do," she said.

"I'm your father," he said. "How could you do this to me?"

"I'm not doing this to you," she said. "I'm doing this for you. You need to be stopped."

Belial reached out to her, but she backed away. "Please," he said. "Don't do this."

"I'm sorry," she said. "But I have to."

She pulled a second dagger from her belt, and Belial closed his eyes, waiting for the inevitable. But the blow never came. Instead, he heard her footsteps walking away. He opened his eyes and saw her disappearing back into the shadows.

Belial slowly pulled the dagger out of his chest. He was wounded, but he was alive. He knew that he had to find Fierna and stop her before she ruined everything. He had to make her understand.

Belial started walking down the ashen road, following the path that Fierna had taken. He didn't know where she was going, but he had a good idea. He walked for hours, following her trail until he came to the entrance to Naome's Tomb. It was a place both of them frequented when they felt lost, unable to determine their next direction.

The mouth of the tomb beckoned to Belial like a lost friend, and he felt a sliver of sorrow course through him as he walked toward the entrance. Naome had been the only one who understood his torment as he struggled to accept what Fate had thrown at him. Sadly, their daughter didn't share the same understanding.

Belial walked up to the door of the sepulcher and laid his hand on the handle. A soft click resounded, and he pushed it open. An acrid stench greeted him as walked down a long hallway to find Fierna on her knees in front of a large sarcophagus.

She heard his soft footsteps approaching and turned to him. "Father," she said. "What are you doing here?"

"I think we need to talk," Belial said. "I want you to understand where I'm coming from."

Fierna looked at her father for a long time, her eyes studying him coldly. Then she finally softened, allowing him a moment to talk to her as father to daughter, instead of an adversary.

"I know that I haven't been a good father," he said. "I've made mistakes, and I've hurt you. But I want you to know that I love you."

"Then why are you trying to leave me?"

Belial searched his mind for a moment, trying to find the right words to say. How could he tell her he longed to go home again, to be where he truly belonged instead of this hellish landscape? Finally, he just said, "I need to go home."

"This is your home, Father."

"No, this place is a prison. I don't belong here."

"Get over yourself, already," Fierna shot back. "With all the shit you've done in the past, Hell is exactly where you belong."

Belial seethed. "Do not pretend to know me, Fierna, or to understand the reason behind my actions."

"Besides the fact that you're an ego-maniac who couldn't handle losing? Did I get it right?"

Belial's eyes flashed with fury as he drew his sword. "You would do well to remember your place, Daughter!" he roared.

Fierna leaped to her feet, her hair erupting into a living mass of fiery tendrils that hissed and spat molten lava. "You're one to talk!" she cried as she hurled a silver dagger at her father's throat.

Belial parried the dagger with his sword, but the force of the blow knocked him off balance. Fierna took advantage of his momentary weakness and lunged at him, her tendrils of flame wrapping around his body in a burning embrace.

Belial struggled to break free, but Fierna's grip was too strong. He could feel the heat of her flames searing his skin, and he knew that if he didn't do something soon, he would be consumed.

With a roar of rage, Belial drove his sword into the ground, using the hilt to pry Fierna's fiery tentacles off his body. As soon as he was free, he lashed out with his sword, slicing through the tentacles and sending them writhing to the ground.

Fierna staggered back, her eyes wide with pain. "You've gone too far this time, Father," she said, her voice trembling with anger.

Belial ignored her. He turned and looked at the stone coffin that had been cracked open by his sword. Inside, the body of his beloved wife lay, her skin as pale as marble and her eyes closed in eternal sleep.

Belial's heart sank. He had lost control in his rage, and now he had defiled the resting place of the only woman he had loved. He fell to his knees, his head in his hands.

"I'm so sorry," he whispered. "I never meant for this to happen."

Fierna stood over him, her eyes filled with hatred. "You're a monster," she said. "I never want to see you again."

And with that, she turned and walked away, leaving Belial alone.

Belial sat there for a long time, staring at the damage he'd done. He had desecrated Naome's tomb, and for that, he could never forgive himself. He felt lost and alone.

Suddenly, there was a gentle touch on his shoulder. He looked up and saw the spirit of his wife standing before him, her dark hair cascading around her shoulders, and a bright smile on her lips.

Belial's eyes widened in surprise. "Naome?" he whispered. For a long moment, he just stared at her, his heart pounding in his chest.

Soft tears gathered in his eyes as his head dropped to his chest. "Please forgive me, my love. Once again, I let my anger control me."

Naome replied, "I'm not the one you should be asking for forgiveness, Belial."

"She'll never understand me like you do."

"She's more like you than you think. She'll come around."

Belial sighed. "I'm not so sure. You know me better than even myself. What should I do?"

Naome reached out and ran her hand softly against his

cheek. "You already know the answer to that. Follow your heart."

"Even if that means leaving you?"

"You know, more than anyone else, that you can never truly leave me. I'll always and forever be a part of you."

Belial reached up and clasped his hand over hers, feeling her soft touch for what he knew would be the last time. "I love you," he said.

"I love you too," she said. And with that, she kissed him gently on the forehead and disappeared.

Chapter 3

Abriymoch stood on the rim of a massive volcano that dominated the landscape. It was a dark and twisted structure of basalt, obsidian, and crystal. This was Belial's place of power, where he ruled over his land cruelly but justly. It was here that he felt the strongest, and as he stood on the balcony that jutted from the throne room, looking into the depths of the flowing lava far below, he began to formulate his plan, knowing that prolonged absence from his domain would weaken him, and could ultimately lead to his demise. He quickly shook that thought from his mind. Death was not an option.

As his mind raced, he paced back and forth on the balcony until frustration began to burn like a fire in his chest. Belial roared out in aggravation, slamming his fist against the wall, sending a crack racing through the stone.

Suddenly, there was a flash of light, and a figure appeared in the doorway. A young woman, dressed in black, with long fiery red hair and intense green eyes, stared at him coolly.

Belial turned to face her. "You're either extremely brave or incredibly foolish. Who are you to enter my fortress uninvited?" he asked threateningly.

"Someone who can help you. I'm Circe," the woman said. "I've seen many things in my lifetime; the rise and fall of empires; the birth and death of gods. And I've seen the end of the world."

Belial's eyes widened. "You know about the end of the world?" he asked.

"Yes," Circe replied. "I know all about it. Granted, it's only one possibility, but it's a strong one, guaranteed to succeed if you play your cards right."

Belial was intrigued. "Tell me everything."

Neither of them noticed Fierna watching from the shadows seething with fury.

***

The parched and fissured land of the Shattered Abyss stretched out before them, a vast wasteland of cracked earth and jagged rocks. The only sound, apart from them, was the wind whistling through the empty spaces, and the only movement was the occasional cloud of dust kicked up by that wind.

Circe led Belial across the barren landscape, her boots crunching on the broken ground. Finally, in the distance, a sinister vortex whirled. As they neared the tempest, the surrounding air grew thick with smoke and dust, and the sound of it was like the roar of a thousand demons. Circe walked with Belial towards the vortex, her eyes fixed on the swirling darkness.

Above them, the sky split open. A dazzling web of lightning bolts snaked down, striking all around them. The ground shook and trembled beneath their feet, while the smell of sulfur overwhelmed their nostrils.

As they reached the eye of the vortex, the shadows swallowed them whole, and they were plunged into darkness. A moment later, they emerged in a hidden cavern deep inside a colossal mountain.

The cavern was lit by a single torch, which cast flickering shadows on the walls. A massive cauldron dominated the cavern, its surface covered in dark bubbles.

Circe's fingers shook as she clutched the four tiny vials, each containing a unique shade of liquid. Belial's eyes burned with fascination as he watched her carefully pour them into the cauldron. The concoction swirled around and then suddenly erupted in an intense burst of light. The cavern glowed with an eerie brilliance; its walls illuminated in an ominous red hue. Everywhere around them, the darkness seemed to vanish, consumed by the enchanting yet sinister luminescence.

Belial grew cautious. "Why are you helping me?"

Circe looked at him, "Let's just say I've been waiting for a long time to see the world above die."

He studied the witch standing before him, judging her intent, then watched as she pulled a silver dagger from her belt and sliced it across her palm, sending a stream of blood pouring out that splashed into the cauldron, mingling its essence with the bubbling liquid.

Raising her arms above her head, Circe began to chant. Her voice, low and guttural, echoed off the walls of the cavern. The flames in the cauldron grew higher and brighter, and the shadows seemed to dance around them.

Belial felt a strange tingling sensation all over his body. He looked down at his hands, and he saw that they were glowing with a faint blue light. He closed his eyes and concentrated, and he felt a surge of power flow through him.

He opened his eyes, and he saw that the cauldron was now filled with a swirling vortex of light.

Circe stopped chanting, and the light from the cauldron began to fade. The shadows in the cavern retreated, and the flames in the cauldron died down. Then Circe was gone, and he was alone in the cavern, standing in front of the cauldron.

He reached out to the cauldron. The surface was cool to the touch, and it felt smooth and polished. He looked down into the cauldron, and saw four vials filled with a swirling silver liquid. Belial picked up the vials and held them in his hand, watching the liquid dance inside each one as if alive.

***

There was a distinct spring in his step when Belial returned to Abriymoch, and immediately made his way downward toward it deepest level. He had hope again. Something he thought was forever dead. Now that he had a plan, one so intricate in its design that it was nearly foolproof, there was no way he could lose.

The asylum was a maze of cells, corridors, and torture chambers, where the inmates were subjected to endless agony and madness. Located deep in the bowels of the stronghold, the screams of the damned echoed through the halls, mingling with the laughter of Belial's twisted servants. It was here that Belial kept his most prized possessions: the souls of the most dangerous criminals. The asylum was his place of horror and madness.

Belial walked eagerly into the main office of the sanatorium and pressed a button on the desk that sent a loud buzz resounding through the room. "Nazur, can you come here, please?"

A nasally voice with a thick German accent responded

immediately. "Right away, Sire!"

A minute later, a short and skinny creature with a bulbous head and long, jutting nose rushed in. He held a clipboard in one hand, cradling it like it was a prized treasure. "You wanted to see me, Sire?"

Belial unrolled a scroll and placed it on a table nearby. The papyrus contained an intricate drawing of an assortment of complex apparatus, all wired together into a morbid closed-circuit television system. "I need this built as soon as possible."

Nazur studied the plans intensely, scribbling notes onto his clipboard at a fevered pace. After a few minutes, he pulled back. "This is quite an interesting display, Sire. May I ask its purpose?"

Belial replied, "Just tell me whether you can build it or not?"

Nazur looked over his notes carefully, flipping pages back and forth. "Of course, Sire. Who do you want to use as a power supply?"

Belial thought for a long moment. He had a few in mind, but hadn't quite decided yet. He needed someone who embodied evil; someone strong and ruthless. "Elizabeth Bathory," he finally said.

Nazur nodded. "A wise choice, Sire. She should work perfectly."

"I don't want a maybe, Nazur!" Belial snapped. "This must succeed!"

Nazur cringed, "My apologies, Sire. It was merely a slip of the tongue. I assure you everything will work perfectly."

"Good. Then I suggest you get to work."

"Of course, Sire. We'll get started immediately."

Belial's eyes followed Nazur's departing figure, then darted around the room eagerly, envisioning the events that would soon unfold to make his scheme a reality. A wicked grin stretched across his face. Everything was falling into place.

Chapter 4

The dirty tile floor of the neglected classroom was stained with muddy footprints and dried spills. A trash can next to the desk at the back of the room was overflowing with crumpled papers, empty bottles, and rotten food. And a musty smell like dirty mop water hung in the air. Maybe that's why Michael was drawn to this place. It felt like home; a place he belonged—neglected and forgotten. Unfortunately, the meetings also pulled a sense of shame and vulnerability from him he didn't enjoy facing. And, God knows, he didn't like talking in front of other people.

Michael perched on one of the chairs that were arranged in a circle in the middle of the room, feeling exposed and vulnerable. His beat-up leather jacket and ripped jeans blended in with the worn and stained outfits of the others. His knee bounced up and down as he fidgeted with his fingers, picking at the loose skin around his nails—both, habits he had developed over the years to cope with his anxiety. His dark hair was disheveled, and his eyes held a haunted presence in them, as if he had seen things no one should ever see.

As he looked around at the group, he saw himself in the reflection of those seated near him. Everyone wore the same cursed and tortured look on their faces. No one wanted to be there, yet all of them knew they needed to be. For some of them, it was the only thing keeping them alive.

The silence was broken by the sound of heels clattering on the floor behind them as Dr. Madison finally walked in. She removed her jacket and laid it across the top of the chair at the head of the group before sitting down. She took a moment to remove a writing pad and pen from her purse and then adjusted her glasses, which reflected her sharp eyes.

The girl sitting next to Michael muttered, "It's about fucking time."

Michael gave a soft chuckle. Lexi's dark demeanor matched the black clothes and make-up she wore perfectly. She wasn't afraid to say what was on her mind, and she didn't care who heard it.

If Dr. Madison heard her, she ignored it and started the meeting right off, "Thank you, everyone, for coming out tonight."

A chorus of mumbles rose from a few of those gathered, but most remained quiet.

"Now, who would like to start things off?" the Doctor continued.

Nearly everyone slunk down in their seats like they were back in school trying to avoid being called on by the teacher.

Then the unthinkable happened. She looked straight at Michael and said the words he dreaded to hear. "What about you, Michael? Would you like to share with the group?"

For a brief second, Michael considered running from the room in fear, but then thought better of it. "Not really," he replied.

A frown covered Dr. Madison's face. "We've talked about this, Michael. You can't heal until you open yourself up and confront your fears."

Michael sighed and resigned himself to his fate, "Okay, fine. My name is Michael, and I'm an addict."

The rest of the group responded in unison, "Hello, Michael."

He took a deep breath. "Not sure what to say since most of you know me, except that every day is a struggle. Has been for a long time."

Various members of the group nodded their heads and murmured words of agreement, both offering their support to each other and revealing their own inner demons.

"How about if you share some of those struggles?" Dr. Madison prodded. "Maybe a few of us can relate?"

Michael hesitated, picking at his fingers again as his knee bounced up and down with greater velocity. Then he finally continued, "I guess it was a few years ago. I don't remember the exact moment, but I know the nightmares started and I couldn't shut them out. They were relentless, attacking me every night until I couldn't take it anymore! I became desperate and realized the only way to quiet them was through drugs and alcohol. Even then, though, I could still feel them, waiting for me in the back of my mind."

Michael paused for a few seconds, trying to find the nerve to continue.

"It's okay, Michael. You're with friends here. Take all the time you need."

He looked around the room. Each one's expression cried out that they understood all too well. The air grew thick with sorrow and hopelessness. He was all too familiar with the well of tears reflected in their eyes. "Eventually, my drug use grew heavier until I found myself in the hospital one day nearly dead. That's when I got clean. At least the first time, anyway."

Michael closed his eyes as he recalled the events of that day. He could still feel the desperation that had surged through him as he rushed into the bathroom and slammed the door. The needle glistened as it slowly pushed into his vein. Seconds later, euphoria flooded through him, vanquishing his darkness. He could breathe again.

The next thing he remembered was being rushed into the hospital on a gurney. As his body convulsed violently, he was dimly aware of the dead man walking behind the group of emergency personnel attending to him. Blood flowed from a bullet hole in his forehead as he reached out to Michael, desperate for help.

Dr. Madison's voice suddenly brought him back to the present. "You're not alone, Michael," she said. "I think it's safe to say that everyone here has had a setback or two in their recovery. The important part is that we keep pushing forward."

A few members of the group murmured their agreement, giving Michael the strength to keep going. "It worked for a while. I stayed clean for nearly six months. The nightmares disappeared, and I finally felt like I had control of my life again. I should've known it wouldn't last."

"And why do you say that?"

"Because, when it happened again, it was worse than before. It felt like my skull was on fucking fire twenty-four-seven, and nothing I did could stop it. I finally tried to end it all myself. If it wasn't for my girlfriend, I wouldn't be here today."

Dr. Madison grew quiet for a moment as she looked at the broken man sitting before them. "I'm sorry, Michael. But I'm glad you're here."

"I wish I could say the same thing," Michael replied.

Dr. Madison looked around the group. "Who else is glad that Michael's here with us today?"

Everyone raised their hand except for Lexi. She jumped to her feet and jabbed a finger at Michael, her expression full of hatred. "What gives you the right to be here, you fucking bastard? You use your 'bad dreams' as an excuse, but the real problem is that you're weak and pathetic. Too weak to even fucking kill yourself the right way!"

Michael looked at Lexi speechless, while Dr. Madison rose from her chair.

"Lexi!" Dr. Madison snapped. "That's no way to talk to Michael. It's not his fault he has no idea what's going on here."

Dr. Madison turned to Michael. Her head shook back and forth vigorously for a few seconds, until the flesh from her face loosened and fell to the floor, revealing a demonic visage underneath. Her red skin glistened with fresh blood, her eyes were black ink wells of the darkest evil, and a wide mouth full of razor-sharp teeth smiled at him. "It's time for you to see what real Hell feels like, Michael!"

Michael screamed as he turned and ran for the door, nearly falling over the chair. The otherworldly snarls and growls behind him told him she wasn't the only Hell-spawned nightmare after him. He heard the other demons behind him scream as they parted ways with their human forms, becoming monsters.

He dashed for his car with a surge of panic, feeling the wind whip his face as he ran faster than he ever thought possible. His heart thudded in his chest and his lungs gasped for air. He was twenty yards from escape, when demonic Lexi flung herself from the second-floor window and landed on the roof of his car, denting it with a loud crunch and sending shards of glass flying.

Michael's only hope for escape now lived in the dense forest surrounding the small, secluded church. Immediately, he changed course and sped forward, hoping to find sanctuary among the trees.

He sprinted through the hellish woods, feeling the razor-sharp claws of branches and vines slicing his skin and splashing his blood on the dark soil. He could hear the demonic hissing and growling of his hunters behind him, closing in on him like a tornado. Suddenly, a monstrous root burst from the ground and ensnared his ankles, hurling him to the forest floor. He barely had time to scream before he was devoured by the beasts. The claws of the demons ripped into Michael's flesh, spilling his blood in a gruesome display.

As Michael cried out, a bright light exploded from him. Angry cries and torturous shrieks flew from the demon's mouths as the light engulfed them. Once it had subsided, he stood up and looked around to find all the members of the group lying on the ground dead, each one back in their original form with their eyes burned out. He dropped to his knees alone and afraid, his soul crying out to be saved from his nightmare.

Dr. Madison's voice suddenly snapped Michael back to reality. "Who else is glad that Michael is here with us today?"

Michael looked around the room in a panic. Everything was back to normal. The demons were gone, their unholy visages replaced by the original group members. Dr. Madison was back to her normal business-like self. Even the musty smell of the classroom returned.

He felt a sudden and intense burning on his right hand. When he looked down, he was shocked to see blood gushing from a deep and jagged wound that slashed the back of his hand, soaking his skin and splattering on the floor. He felt a surge of fear and pain, and without thinking, he leaped from his chair and bolted from the room, his face contorted in horror.

Michael rushed down the hall toward the small bathroom at the end and burst through the door. Blood turned the white porcelain of the sink a bright shade of red for a moment before the water from the faucet washed it down the drain.

As he ran the cut under the water, he looked at his reflection in the mirror. For a split second, the scene changed, and he saw the bodies on the ground again, smoke rising in a steady stream from the earth surrounding them, their hollow eyes screaming at him, asking him why? Then the reflection returned to normal.

Michael clung to the sink's edge, his chest heaving as he wept bitterly. He felt a surge of despair wash over him, drowning him in sorrow. As the darkness flooded over him, he wondered how long before it consumed it completely?

Chapter 5

In the dimly lit corner of the drab diner, Michael nervously twirled the fork in his hand, avoiding Mary's piercing gaze. She looked weary and unhappy, her eyes shadowed by insomnia and her mouth set in a thin line of displeasure. He felt a pang of guilt as he realized how much he had put her through. *She's so tired,* he thought. *All because of me.*

Mary sensed his anxiety rising and changed the subject, "How was group today?"

Michael stared at the table, where his fingers drummed nervously. He wished he could hide his inner turmoil from her, but he felt like she could see right through him. "It was fine," he said as he moved the silverware around absently.

She eyed him for a second, knowing he was full of shit. "Did you share anything?"

"A little bit."

"That's good. Opening up helps."

Michael grew silent as the server showed up and placed their food in front of them, thankful to have a sudden distraction from her questioning.

"Anything else?" the waitress asked in an obviously disinterested tone.

Mary replied, "No, thank you," and the girl walked away from the table, leaving them in silence for a minute.

When Michael picked up a French fry, Mary noticed the cut on his hand. "Shit! That looks like it hurts. How'd you do that?"

Michael looked at his hand for a second. The skin was red and irritated, as infection started to set in, an infection that was spreading far deeper than he'd ever let her know.

He brushed it off as nothing, refusing to pour more worry on top of the only person who had ever truly loved him back. "Must've happened after group," he said matter-of-factly. "I guess I brushed against something sharp."

As Michael grabbed another French fry, Mary tried her best to hide her worry. She knew it was a futile attempt, and she cursed herself silently for caring so much for the broken man in front of her.

The rest of the meal was eaten in silence and was followed by a car ride just as cold. Any conversation would feel like empty words voiced simply for the sake of saying them, and both of them were so tired.

After the walk from the parking lot to his apartment door, Mary stood beside him, her eyes still holding a hint of concern. "Are you sure you don't want me to come in?"

"Nah, you've got to get up early for work," Michael replied. "I'll be okay."

Mary reached up and stroked the side of his face, rubbing her hand over the rough stubble bristling across his cheek. "You need to shave. You look like shit."

Michael quipped, "Gee, thanks. You're a little rough around the edges too."

Mary knew what he was doing. Making little jokes was his

way of ignoring his problems. Finally, she gave in, "Okay, you win. But if you need me, you call. Got it?"

"Loud and clear."

He smiled a big, fake smile and then gave her a soft kiss before he unlocked the door and went inside.

Mary lingered for a brief minute before she walked back out of the apartment building, worry still clouding her face. She knew he wouldn't be okay, and she also knew he wouldn't call.

***

Michael sighed as he tossed his keys onto the small table nearby and stood for a while with his back against the door, his face a picture of guilt. He hated lying to Mary, but he was so afraid of losing her he believed he had no other choice. If she knew what was really happening to him, she'd leave him for sure.

It had started a long time ago, these episodes of madness when the master of dreams invaded his sleep. His visits always left Michael cold and shaking as he struggled to hold on to his last sliver of humanity. Morning could never come soon enough, when the light of the sun vanquished the horror, at least temporarily, and he could live again. But even during the day, he could feel the nightmares skulking in the shadows, just out of reach.

Michael sat down on the couch and reached for the bottle of caffeine pills on the end table. He was determined not to let the nightmares in, even if it meant staying up all night. A hint of shame passed through his eyes as he popped a couple in his mouth, downing them with a long swig from an energy drink. Then he grabbed the remote and turned on the TV.

Already exhausted from his ordeal at the church, his

eyelids got heavy sooner than expected. Michael popped a few more pills into his mouth, hoping to stay the darkness.

The effects only lasted a short time before he got sleepy again. Tears ran down his face as he cried out, "No, no, no! Please, God, help me! I can't take this anymore!"

As he had done so many times recently, he turned to an old friend with a desperate plea for salvation. "I'm sorry, Mary," he sputtered as the needle found the vein readily, and he breathed a sigh when the White Lady worked her magic quickly.

But even her salvation didn't last, and before long he was feverishly fighting the mind demon, repeatedly sending it scurrying back into the shadows. But his body was weak and a wave of panic set in. He tried to calm himself down, but his brain wouldn't cooperate. Instead of finding peace, all he found was madness. His throat burned as he gasped in gulps of air, trying to keep up with the demand of his pounding heart.

Then, almost as if a switch had been thrown, his body shut down. He couldn't go any further. His breathing eased, his heartbeat steadied, and the lead weights that hung on his eyelids found their way to the bottom of his pupils. The last words to roll off his tongue before darkness overtook him were, "Fuck me!"

Chapter 6

Julie gazed at herself in the bathroom mirror and felt a lump in her throat. She didn't recognize the woman staring back at her anymore. The dark circles under her eyes were so deep and persistent that they looked like bruises. Her skin was pale and dull, and her hair was a messy bun with strands of it sticking out wildly. In short, she looked like someone who had given up on life.

"How did everything get so fucked up?" she said to her reflection.

When her other self didn't answer, she sighed.

Her perfect life with the man of her dreams was gone, along with the hope of the family that she'd never have. And she was to blame. Maybe not directly, but there was no one else to shoulder it. Tom certainly didn't.

She lifted the front of her shirt and rubbed her stomach lightly, closing her eyes and trying to imagine what it would be like to have a life growing inside her. It had almost happened. More than once. But almost doesn't count. Not when life is concerned.

The mirror image shifted abruptly. She was sitting in a wheelchair, dressed in a hospital gown, with Tom, her overbearing husband who stood a head taller than her, pushing her through the hospital with a determined grip. Above them, the florescent lights hummed and blinked, creating a harsh contrast between light and shadow.

They raced through the dark hall, where every door concealed a secret. Behind them, screams of terror and pain echoed from the rooms, where unspeakable things awaited. They rounded a corner and faced a nurse's station, where three nurses stared blankly at them. Their scrubs were splattered with blood and their faces were covered by plastic masks that had twisted smiles painted on them.

"She's about ready to pop, ladies!" Tom said eagerly. "Let's hope for success this time."

The nurses led them to a nearby room, where Tom shoved the wheelchair over to a bed covered with blood-stained sheets and a thin pillow. Two of the nurses grabbed Julie roughly from the wheelchair and wrenched her onto the bed, while the third nurse fiddled with the bed's controls to tilt the head of the bed up.

Julie's scream pierced the air as a wave of pain seared her body. Tom clasped Julie's hand and felt her pulse racing, trying to comfort her with his touch.

"It won't be long now, dear," Tom reassured her.

Minutes later, a doctor came in wearing a plague doctor mask and sat down on a rusty stool at the foot of the bed. He pushed Julie's legs back hard, bringing a cry of pain from her, and extended the stirrups from their compartments, propping her feet up.

Julie shrieked in agony, feeling another contraction rip her apart. The doctor yanked Julie's gown up to her navel, revealing her bulging belly. He probed her with his fingers and his gaze, then nodded to the nurses, indicating that the moment had come.

The nurses rushed over, pushing a cart full of surgical instruments. The doctor looked at the cart and then at Tom, pointing to Julie's abdomen.

"Apparently, he needs he needs to perform a C-section to remove the baby," Tom interpreted.

Julie looked at Tom worriedly, who responded with acid in his voice, "Nothing is ever easy with you, is it? Why can't you just be like other women and deliver a normal baby?"

Tom turned toward the doctor and threw his hands up in exasperation, "Oh well, just do it already!"

As the nurses pinned Julie's arms and legs to the bed, trapping her like a helpless animal, the doctor snatched a scalpel from the cart and slashed Julie's stomach. She wailed in horror and pain as a gush of blood spurted from her.

Julie was on the verge of unconsciousness as the doctor plunged his hands into her stomach, his fingers writhing around her insides, before he pulled the baby from her. Tom followed the doctor as he carried the baby to the corner of the room.

But something was wrong. The doctor looked at the nurses, then at Tom, and shook his head.

Julie struggled through blurry eyes to see them standing in the corner, Tom talking animatedly to the doctor. His voice was only a series of sharp hisses in her ears.

"What's wrong?" Julie asked weakly, fearing the worst. "Why can't I see my baby?"

Tom approached the bed carrying their newborn baby boy, dangling him upside down by one leg. He tossed the baby onto Julie's chest.

"Another abject failure, Julie!" Tom spat. "Why am I not surprised? What is that, four now?"

Julie looked at her stillborn son on her chest. His skin was blue and mottled, one of his hands was deformed, and his chest cavity was caved in.

"No!" she cried out before the scene abruptly shifted back to normal. It was a nightmare that had visited her nearly every day since, and it would likely continue to do so until her last breath. It had become ingrained in her mind and her soul.

She felt a wave of tears crashing over her eyes and she quickly dropped her shirt before curling up on the floor, where she gave up and wept silently. Not a full-fledged cry, though, so that Tom would hear her. The last thing she needed was to listen to him telling her to get over it and move on. In his eyes, her miscarriages had simply been medical emergencies. And like any other medical procedure, it took time to heal. He didn't understand the mental scars left behind.

It was the last one, three years ago, that had driven the biggest wedge into their relationship. Tom slowly distanced himself from her. He looked at her differently, no longer holding her in his eyes with the same twinkle she had fallen in love with. And he rarely touched her anymore, avoiding any sense of sexual advance from her like she was infested by the plague or something.

She felt alone in her marriage and wondered why they were even still together. But she knew the answer to that. For Tom, divorce equaled failure. And he never failed at anything. It wasn't in his nature.

When they had first met, she categorized this as his drive to succeed. But now she recognized it to be simply his controlling nature. He was—and would always be—right about everything.

As a result, she had let herself go a bit. She wasn't obese or anything, but she certainly wasn't the same woman anymore that used to turn heads when she walked into a room.

A light tapping on the bathroom door shook Julie momentarily from her depressive thoughts before Tom called from the other side. "Julie? Are you okay in there?"

She wiped her eyes dry and stood up. "Yeah, I'm fine."

"I thought I heard you crying."

"No, I'm okay. It's just allergies. They've been kicking my ass all day. I'll be out in a minute," she answered.

Tom was silent for a moment. "You're not having another episode, are you?" he asked with a hint of malice in his voice.

"No, I'm fine," she lied.

"Well, just hurry up. Dinner's almost ready."

Julie opened the medicine cabinet and rifled through the pills for a moment before she found a bottle of Xanax. She popped one into her mouth and bent under the faucet to down it with a quick gulp of water.

Then she blew her nose, flushed the toilet, and left the room.

Julie slunk out of the bathroom with her head down low to avoid Tom's gaze. As she passed by, Tom grabbed her arm. "You've been crying, haven't you?" he accused.

"I told you I'm fine," she said as she pulled away from him.

A grunt escaped Tom's lips as he let her go and watched her walk away, disgust clear in his eyes.

Chapter 7

Julie sat alone at the table, wrapped in a blanket of sorrow and despair, when Sampson jumped up and rubbed against her hand, purring softly. She gently stroked the black fur on his head and scratched that special spot under his chin. She looked into his mysterious eyes and saw the kind of arcane knowledge hidden inside that only a cat possesses reflected at her.

"You always know how to make me feel better, Samps, don't you?" she said as she continued to caress his soft fur.

Sampson pushed his head into her hand, begging for more attention.

"I feel so lost right now. What am I going to do?"

Sampson replied with a soft meow.

"You're the only one that understands what I'm going through."

The chandelier over the table flickered for a second as Tom entered the room carrying two plates of food. Sampson growled and hissed for a moment before he jumped from the table and scampered out of the room.

Tom placed a plate of food in front of Julie before he sat down across from her with his own plate. "You know I don't like him on top of the table," he said as he unfolded a napkin and placed it on his lap.

Julie didn't answer.

Tom looked at her and frowned. "Should I make an appointment with Dr. Andrews?"

Julie shook her head slowly. "No. I'll be fine. I just need some rest."

Tom stared at her quietly for a moment, before starting into his meal. "Okay. I made your favorite: baked salmon with a honey glaze on top of a bed of rice pilaf."

"It looks wonderful," she replied half-heartedly.

On a normal day, Julie could appreciate the intricacies involved in preparing what he would describe as his signature dish. This dish was one of her favorites. But today was different. Today was hard. It would've been her son's third birthday, a fact that had been lost on Tom a long time ago. And as that thought manifested inside her, she grew even more despondent, her depression taking hold of her with a stronger grip than ever before. As a result, her appetite had disappeared.

Tom watched her picking at her food and frowned. "Aren't you going to eat?" he asked her, though it was more of a statement than a question.

Julie replied, "I'm sorry. I'm not very hungry. I haven't been feeling too well."

"Ah, yes, your allergies again," Tom said in an accusatory tone that suggested he didn't believe her.

His eyes flashed with malice as he fixed her with a ruthless and sinister stare. She felt a surge of terror when he roared at her in a deafening voice, slamming his fist down on the table in front of hm. "I don't give one flying fuck about your damn allergies! I spent hours slaving in the kitchen to prepare this dinner for you, and you're going to fucking eat it, whether you want to or not!"

Tom vaulted out of his seat and rushed at her, holding a knife and fork in his hands menacingly. Standing directly behind her, he pushed her chair to the edge of the table with enough force that a cry issued from her lips as he pinned her arms to her side. He acted like a man possessed, frantically shoveling food into her mouth without giving her a chance to chew or swallow before he shoved the next bite in. "This'll teach you to be a little more grateful next time!"

When she began to choke and gag, it only fueled his anger further. "Don't make me do something I might regret," he spat.

He ignored her desperate attempts to free herself from his grasp, as her body began to tremble while she fought to breathe. Instead, he held up the knife with a large piece of fish attached to the end. "Last bite, and you're all done," he said.

When she tried to pull back one last time, he jammed the knife into her mouth with enough force that the tip of the blade tore through the back of her throat and continued until it extended out of her neck, sending a spray of blood covering the back of the chair and the floor below. For a brief second, her brain screamed, '*Why?*' before everything went dark.

A moment later, Tom's voice brought her back from the madness, "Ah, yes, your allergies again."

Julie looked around in shock for a moment.

"What's wrong, Julie?" Tom asked.

Julie was frantic, as she searched for words, "I... I don't...Something's happening. I don't know what's going on?"

She jumped up from her chair and ran out of the room

37

filled with terror.

"Aren't you going to eat?" Tom asked as she disappeared from view.

Tom shook his head, a look of scorn plastered on his face, as he resumed his own meal.

***

Julie lay on her bed with Sampson snuggled next to her. Her eyes red and puffy from crying. She rubbed his head gently, bringing a soft comforting meow from him.

"He wasn't always like this, Samps. It feels like a lifetime ago, but there was a time when we were happy."

A flurry of images flew into her brain, memories of happier times. First, they were running alone the beach on a bright sunny day, laughing and kicking sand at each other as the surf drifted in and out. Then, they were enjoying a romantic picnic in the park, birds and squirrels squawking like nosy neighbors gossiping. And then, their wedding night, the night they became one, in mind, body, and soul, forever. Or so she had thought.

As the images faded from her mind, she tried to cling to them feebly, hoping somehow to manifest them back into her life. But she knew she would never get them back.

"I know he blames me," she sighed. "And I'm beginning to think he's right. Something's broken inside me that can't be fixed. And, now I feel like I'm losing my mind."

She looked at Sampson sadly. "What am I going to do?"

Sampson snuggled closer to her.

"At least you love me, right?"

Sampson replied with a soft meow.

With a sigh, Julie closed her eyes and drifted off to sleep. As she straddled between the waking world and dream realm, she heard a chorus of children's voices singing, their haunting voices echoing to her from the ether, *'London bridge is falling down, falling down, falling down. London bridge is falling down, my fair lady.'*

Then darkness overtook her completely.

Chapter 8

The darkness in the room was all-encompassing, covering Julie in a blanket of sorrow and despair. As she tossed and turned in a restless and troubled sleep, a baby's cry suddenly jolted her awake. She jumped from the bed in a panic, and rushed into the hallway, where the single cry became a chorus, echoing around her from all directions.

The corridor was long and dark, with doors along both sides. Desperately, she threw open each one to look into a nursery with a solitary crib in the center of the room, but when she rushed forward to rescue the crying baby, the crib was empty. Back and forth, she repeated her desperate search, and each time was met with the same result.

Then, she came to the end of the hallway, where a final door waited. When she reached for the handle, the crying suddenly stopped.

Slowly, Julie inched her way inside. The room was larger than the others, with stone walls lit by an array of candles perched atop iron sconces. Dark shadows in the corners whispered in hushed tones barely audible. The center of the room was filled by a raised platform with a wooden cradle resting on top.

Sampson was on the floor next to the platform, scratching and clawing feverishly at something. Julie bent down and whispered, "Quiet, Sampson! You're going to wake him up!"

Sampson turned toward her, hissing and growling as if she were threatening to snatch away his prized possession.

Julie backed away from him in shock and he turned back around to focus once again on the subject in front of him.

Shaken at his reaction, Julie turned toward the cradle, and this time, found a small baby lying quietly inside. She picked up the child gently and held him to her chest, rocking him softly. After a minute, she tilted the baby forward so she could see his face. When she saw the blueish tint to his skin and his still chest, she sobbed. "No! Not again!"

As she slunk to her knees in quiet despair, something squished under her. She looked around to see the floor littered with unborn fetuses in various stages of development. The dead baby in her arms suddenly melted into a pile of blood and bones. Sampson turned to her with his mouth clamped tightly onto the umbilical cord of one of the unborn children.

Julie jumped back to her feet and tried to run for the door, but the floor had become as slick as oil and she fell backward, hitting her head on the floor.

The shadows in the room grew darker, the whispers louder, as long, bony figures closed in on her.

As her consciousness left her, tears streamed down her face while a baby's cry sounded off in the distance once more. She knew it was her baby boy crying for her, and she knew she couldn't save him.

***

The alarm clock buzzed loudly, waking Julie from her nightmare. She sat up, trembling for a minute as the images faded from her mind until she could breathe again. They were getting worse, and she didn't know what to do. Talking to Tom was out of the question. *Hell, he'd probably have me committed.* She remembered the episode at the dinner table the previous night and started crying softly. *Maybe that's where I belong?*

She sighed as she reached over and banged the top of the clock to hit the snooze button before flopping back down onto her pillow. For a minute, she stared at the ceiling, letting the emptiness engulf her and closed her eyes.

The phone jolted her awake sometime later. She looked at the clock and shot out of bed. It was already nine-thirty, and she was late for work! She knew who was on the other end of the phone and didn't answer.

"Shit!" she said as she rifled through her closet, looking for something to wear. "The boss is gonna kill me."

After dressing in record time, she rushed into the bathroom, and quickly put her hair in a bun, frantically brushed some foundation on her cheeks, then licked the end of the toothpaste tube. She looked at herself in the mirror and frowned. "You really fucked up this time, Jules!"

As Julie grabbed her keys and purse from the small table next to the front door, she saw a briefcase on the floor. *That's odd. I thought Tom had a meeting today?*

When she reached for the door handle, Sampson scampered into the room, jumped up on the table, and meowed at her softly, looking for attention.

"Sorry, Samps. I can't right now," she said, glancing down

at the briefcase once more on her way out the door.

The tires squealed loudly as she put the car in reverse and stepped on the gas. Her recklessness almost cost her more than she bargained for, as she barely avoided hitting a young man riding his bike, sending him crashing to the ground as he dodged the collision. She slammed on her brakes and sat there, shaken for a minute, before continuing.

Of course, while on her way to work, she hit every red light imaginable. "Fuck!" she cried out as she had to stop yet again. As soon as the light turned green, she stepped on the gas and sped through the intersection.

Seconds later, she saw those horrible flashing lights in her rear-view mirror. "Shit, now what?"

After pulling over to the curb, she looked in the side mirror and watched as a woman in a police uniform approached her car. As she drew near, her sunglasses reflected brightly in her mirror, causing Julie to squint for a second. A soft tap told her to roll down her window.

Julie looked up worriedly. "Is there something wrong, officer?" she mumbled.

The officer responded in a stern voice, "License and registration, please."

Julie's hands trembled as she fumbled through her purse for her license. Then she flipped down her visor, where she kept her registration.

The officer snatched these out of Julie's hand and studied them silently for a moment before speaking again.

"Julie Dunbar?"

"Yes," she replied softly.

The officer grew quiet for a moment before speaking. "Do you have any idea why I pulled you over?"

Julie swallowed hard. "To be honest, officer, I'm not sure."

A small grin played on the officer's face as she looked at

the scared woman in the driver's seat. "I'll be back in a minute." She abruptly turned around and walked back to her car.

Julie sat there nervously as the minutes ticked by. *The boss is gonna understand. Hell, he probably won't even notice,* she kept telling herself over and over to convince herself that her professional career wasn't about to completely go to shit.

A loud metallic whisper squelched through the car's radio, causing Julie to jump. As she reached over to turn the knob, she was surprised to find it already turned off.

A tap on the glass startled her again. Julie rolled her window down and the officer handed her documents back. She looked down at Julie over the tops of her glasses. "Have a nice day, Mrs. Dunbar. And be careful. Someone might get hurt."

Julie sat in shock as she watched the police car speed away. Not once had the officer alluded to why she had been pulled over. A little voice in the back of her mind whispered that something wasn't quite right.

After a minute, she regained her composure and continued to work. She turned hastily into the parking lot, only to find it completely full. Mondays at Price Accounting Firm were normally quiet, but today was certainly an exception to the rule.

"You'd think there was some kind of convention in town," she exclaimed as she circled the lot twice before she found an empty parking spot that she was sure wasn't there a minute ago. Quickly, she grabbed her briefcase and rushed to the front door.

The receptionist, Tammy, a dour old woman with horn-rimmed glasses, glanced irritatingly at the clock as Julie rushed in. "Late again," she hissed.

Julie ignored her as she rushed across the lobby toward the

elevator, where she felt Tammy's judging eyes on her as she waited. Finally, a loud beep signaled the opening of the doors. As she entered the small chamber and pressed the button to go to the fifth floor, an evil smile spread across Tammy's face, her features taking on a sinister look, like someone who delighted in tormenting helpless animals.

As the elevator door closed tight and lurched upward, Julie shook her head to remove Tammy's image from her mind. She thought of Tom, and how disappointed he would be if he saw her now. He was always the consummate professional and highly frowned on poor work habits from his subordinates. It was measurably worse with his wife.

The overhead light flickered briefly before steadying. A screech reverberated through the speaker in the ceiling, and the soft elevator music was replaced with a chorus of creepy children's voices. *'Iron bars will bend and break, bend and break, bend and break. Iron bars will bend and break, my fair lady.'*

She heard a soft whisper in her ear, "Julie."

Julie spun around to find the elevator empty.

When she reached the fifth floor, she quietly exited the elevator, shaken from the dark voice resounding in her head, and headed toward her office, slinking low, hoping to sneak in without being noticed.

No such luck.

Seconds later, the phone in her office rang. Julie's hands were trembling as she picked up the handset. Her heart sank when Mr. Price's husky voice sounded on the other end, "Julie, I need to see you in my office immediately."

"Yes, Sir," she replied softly.

With a thick lump forming in her throat, Julie dragged her feet along the dreaded corridor that led to Mr. Price's office, a destination she had visited too often in the past few months. She felt the cold sweat on her palms and the knot in her stomach. She knew she was walking on a razor's edge.

At last, Julie came to the large oak door that led to Mr. Price's office and took a deep breath before knocking.

The disappointment in Mr. Price's words made her cringe. "Come in," he said tersely.

The big man refused to look up from the reports stacked in front of him as Julie entered the office, and merely pointed absently at the chair in front of the desk. "Have a seat," he said.

Julie sat down and crossed her legs, watching anxiously as Mr. Price continued with his paperwork, letting her stew in quiet agony for a moment. Finally, he looked up and surveyed her quietly for a moment before speaking. "How long have you worked here, Julie?"

She swallowed hard as a bead of sweat formed on her brow. "Almost three years," she answered softly.

"And in those three years, how many times have you been late for work?"

She was quiet for a moment before speaking. "I know I've been late a few times, Mr. Price, but I'm trying really hard. It's just that Tom and I are having some problems right now and I haven't been sleeping well at night. But I'll do better, I promise."

The expression on Mr. Price's face remained unchanged. "To be quite honest, Julie, your situation at home is of little concern to me. What matters to me is the fact that you're not at your job when you're supposed to be."

Julie started shaking, causing her voice to crack as she spoke. "But you have to admit I do a good job when I'm here."

"Listen to the last part of that statement, Julie—when I'm here. That's the real problem. How can you do your job if you're not here? It's not fair to everyone else that comes to work on time and prepared."

"But, Mr. Price, I swear I'll do better. Please, give me one more chance."

"I'm sorry, Julie. You're out of chances. It's time to relieve you of your duties. You have one hour to clear out your desk and remove your belongings. Security will then escort you from the building. Have a nice day."

Chapter 9

Michael found himself in the driver's seat of a Thunderbird convertible, with Mary sitting in the passenger's seat next to him, speeding along a desert road.

Michael looked at Mary terrified. "Where are we? What the hell's going on?"

A chorus of sirens filled the air from a squad of police cars chasing them.

"Don't you remember?" Mary asked.

"Remember what?"

"You killed a man, Michael!"

Michael's heart raced. The tires screeched as he jerked the car around a hairpin turn in the road, leaving a trail of dust behind him.

"That can't be true!" Michael exclaimed. "I could never kill anyone."

Mary replied, "It was that prick from the shop. You said you got into a fight when he came back to get his car."

Michael struggled to recall the incident, then a scene started playing out in his head: He was working in the shop, arguing with an angry customer. A couple of cars sat in nearby stalls with their hoods up and engines running, while the other service techs watched the argument.

"Things got out of hand and he hit you," Mary continued, "but, when you hit him back, he spun around and staggered onto the motor of a nearby car."

Michael saw the argument escalating in his brain—or at least what he imagined could've happened—both men yelling and cursing at each other, until punches were thrown. Michael connected with a hard blow to the man's jaw that spun him around so that he staggered backward. It happened so fast that the other mechanic didn't have a chance to stop the man's face from hitting the fan blade, sending a spray of blood onto the engine, causing it to hiss and smoke. Then the hood smashed down on the man, killing him.

"I don't remember any of that!" Michael cried frantically. "Why don't I remember?"

A barrage of bullets suddenly hit the rear of the car. Mary reached under the seat and pulls up a gun.

Michael's eyes grew wide. "Where in the fuck did you get a gun?" he cried.

Mary replied simply, "It was under the seat. Must've belonged to the guy you killed."

"Will you stop saying that!"

Mary turned around in her seat and fired at the police cars chasing them, her eyes holding the crazed look of an escaped convict running for their life. After a few shots, she turned back around. "You know I love you, no matter what, right?"

Michael looked at her fearfully, his heart beating a million miles a minute. "I love you too."

He felt a surge of panic when he looked forward and realized they were running out of road. As they got closer to the edge of a massive canyon, Michael spun his head around wildly, trying to find an escape. The roar of the wind and the rumble of the engine beat in his brain like a drum corps, while the smell of smoke and dust choked off his breath as the abyss loomed ahead.

"Keep going, Michael!" Mary ordered.

"But...there's nowhere to go!" Michael cried frantically.

He turned his head to find Mary pointing the gun at him. "For once in your fucking life, Michael, do what you're told! I said keep going!"

Michael gripped the steering wheel tight as they neared the edge of the cliff. He looked at her sadly, tears welling up in his eyes. "I'm sorry."

"I know," Mary replied softly.

She grabbed Michael's hand and held it tight as they plummeted off the cliff into the hungry mouth of the chasm. As they soared through the air, the grip on Michael's hand tightened like a vise, crunching his bones, and causing him to cry out.

Michael looked over in agony and saw Belial sitting there.

Belial looked at him coldly. His eyes were like ice, but full of rage. "I don't know who the fuck you think you are, but you don't belong here! Get out!"

A violent blow to the side of the head sent Michael spiraling out of the falling car toward the jagged rocks below. "And don't interrupt me again!" Belial bellowed. The words echoed throughout the canyon in a dire warning.

But, as Michael's face was about to meet the rocky floor, the ground opened up and he fell through the ceiling of an office building and crashed to the floor. After a minute, he dragged himself up and looked around, completely dazed.

The sign behind the receptionist's desk told him he was in an accounting firm. The figure behind the desk told him he was in Hell. A sketchy version of a woman sat in the chair posing as a receptionist, but Michael's eyes saw her as something different—a ghastly skeletal figure resembling the image seen from an x-ray machine. Her outline shimmered like a specter as she moved, while her empty black eye sockets regarded him coldly. A hideous, fleshless grin spread across the demon's skull.

The demonic receptionist's eyes widened in delight as Julie suddenly burst through the front door and raced through the lobby. The receptionist's lips curled into a cruel sneer, and she let out a high-pitched shriek that echoed through the building as if she were a lookout announcing Julie's arrival.

Julie sprinted across the lobby, her heels clicking against the marble floor. She reached the elevator and jabbed at the button, but the doors refused to open. "Don't do this to me!" Julie muttered as she hit the button again repeatedly.

The receptionist's face was twisted into a mask of hatred, her eyes were glowing with a malevolent light, as she turned toward Michael. She raised her hand and made a slashing gesture across her throat, sending a chill down his spine.

Seconds later, Michael was standing outside the elevator on the fifth floor. As he glanced around, he saw that everyone there had the same skeletal figure, the same shimmering outline, and the same evil grin as the receptionist downstairs.

The elevator opened and Michael watched as a dark, writhing shadow emerged with the woman following unsuspectingly behind. As the wraith passed in front of Michael, it turned and looked at him with its gaping blackness, as if to say, "Watch this!"

Michael followed them down a long hallway that had numerous doors on either side, each with a small window tucked in the center. A damp and foul odor permeated the place—a mixture of mold and mildew, coupled with the unmistakable scents of urine and feces. Tortured screams reverberated all around.

Periodically, he heard a loud slam from the other side of one door, and then he would catch a quick glimpse of someone, or something, pressed up against the tiny window pane, pleading for an escape that wouldn't come.

Julie entered one room and Michael glimpsed the wraith standing behind her, with its bony fingers wrapped around her neck. Dark whispers echoed through the room.

Michael cried, "Behind you!" but the door slammed shut. He tried to move forward, but a dozen black and gnarled claws shot through the floor and grabbed his legs, immobilizing him.

A moment later, Julie exited the office and walked solemnly down the hall. The shadow of the wraith now engulfed her, like dark spiderwebs, encircling her body.

The claws released their grip on Michael, allowing him to follow.

Finally, they came to the end of the hallway, where a large stone door stood with a symbol engraved on it—a circle within a circle, and a strange-looking skull in its center, with a series of six letters written in an unknown language spaced equally around the outside ring. Even though he couldn't read them, Michael knew immediately that the letters spelled out the name of the demon tormenting his dreams.

When the door creaked open, he saw the same man from the car sitting behind the desk with a wide grin on his face. Michael made a move to rush in after the woman, but two of the shimmering specters grabbed him. "Not so fast, pretty boy," one creature said in a clickety voice, "You're in our world now."

A loud clanking noise echoed down the hallway, and Michael watched in horror as a gang of skeletal figures pushed a beat-up gurney toward him. He felt the warmness of fresh blood and bodily fluids on his back from a recent occupant as they slammed him onto the top of the apparatus. Seconds later, he was bound hand and foot to the metal railing, with another strap crossing his chest. Then, he was whisked back down the hall, where a door stood open, waiting eagerly for him.

The overhead lights flickered like an overactive disco ball as they wheeled him inside, making it hard to focus. A chorus of anxious hisses flooded the room, and it was only when they raised the back of the gurney to an upright position that he could see the source of the insane noise. The floor of the room was filled with serpents of all kinds—rattlesnakes, cobras, vipers, copperheads—each one coiled and ready to strike.

A minute later, the woman walked past the open doorway with her head held high and her face set it a firm resolve that is often seen on a death-row inmate walking toward the gas chamber, ready to accept their fate. Michael knew that inside this woman was lost and damaged.

The dream demon followed closely behind her, but when he came to the door, he stepped inside and approached Michael, with the sea of serpents slithering aside as if he were Moses parting the Red Sea.

"I see you're still trying to interfere," he spat. "What makes you so special that you think you can stop me?"

He uttered a sharp command and a pair of vipers slithered up his legs and curled around his body until their heads rested in his hands. "This should make you think twice about meddling where you don't belong!"

Two of the specters removed the straps around Michael's wrists and turned his hands over to reveal the main arteries on each one. Another sharp command and the vipers lunged forward, embedding their fangs deep into Michael's flesh.

Michael cried out as the venom shot through his system, causing his veins to bulge and pulsate before they turned black and dark puss started oozing from them.

Belial laughed. "You're nothing but a broken man with a broken soul. You're a failed attempt at a human being, weak and pathetic."

A stream of foam bubbled from Michael's mouth as he fought against the poison burning his body from the inside. Then everything went dark.

Chapter 10

Julie felt a surge of pain in her chest and a lump in her throat as she fought to keep the tears from spilling. She ran into her office and shut the door behind her before she collapsed into a heap of misery. She pressed her face into her hands on her desk as she wept, wondering how her life had fallen apart.

She was sure Tom would be disappointed. Hopefully, he would be supportive. Financially, they'd be okay for a while until she found another job. But who would hire her now with this attendance record hanging over her like a dark cloud?

A soft knock on the door interrupted her tears. "Come in," she said.

It was Andrew, the security officer, a nice man in his forties, with light brown hair and a mustache. "I'm sorry to hear about your termination, Ma'am."

That word made her flinch—termination. It sounded so violent; so final. "It's alright, Andrew. I guess I only have myself to blame."

"Still, I'm going to miss seeing your smile every day. Most

of the other women around here are total bitches."

Julie chuckled. "Thanks, Andrew. You always have a way of cheering everyone up. Just give me another minute and I'll be ready to go."

She grabbed an empty box from the corner of her office and haphazardly threw the contents of her desk inside. When she topped the stack off with a picture of Tom and her happy together, she stopped and stared at it longingly, her eyes misting over once more. Then she flicked off the light switch and followed Andrew down the hall.

A few heads turned as they headed toward the elevator. Some of them showed signs of sadness for her; while others were ecstatic that she'd been fired. None of that mattered to her now. Julie's only concern was how Tom was going to handle the news. The last thing she needed right now was to disappoint him yet again.

As Julie and Andrew stepped inside the elevator, the light overhead flickered for a brief second. Andrew looked up at the ceiling and frowned.

"Are you sure you're going to be okay, Ma'am?" Andrew asked.

Conviction was lacking in Julie's voice, contradicting her words, "Yeah, I'll be okay. I'm just not sure how Tom will take the news? He hasn't been quite himself lately."

"Hopefully, he'll understand and be supportive."

"To be honest with you, Andrew, I don't know if he will?"

"Well, if all else fails, you can put your trust in God to help you through this tough time."

Julie looked at him pointedly. "Not to be rude, Andrew, but that ship sailed a long time ago."

The ding of the elevator when it reached the first floor was a death knell for Julie. Andrew led the way as they exited and headed toward the entrance. Tammy enthusiastically waved goodbye as they passed by her desk.

"Bye, Hun," Tammy said. "I would say, have a nice life, but I have a feeling I'll be seeing you again real soon."

Andrew shot Tammy a stern look that immediately made her shift in her seat uncomfortably and look away.

As Andrew escorted her out of the building toward her car, Julie noticed eerily that the parking lot was now completely deserted.

Julie stopped as she was about to climb into her car and turned to Andrew.

"Listen, I'm sorry about the comment I made in the elevator."

"Don't worry about it, Ma'am," Andrew replied. "I was just trying to give you a little hope."

Julie sighed. "That's certainly something I could use right now."

She tossed the box from the office onto the backseat, then got into her car and turned on the ignition, sitting there for a few minutes in quiet contemplation. *What am I going to do?*

She thought about calling Tom at work and telling him what had happened. Maybe he'd take the rest of the day off, and they could have some quiet time to figure out what to do next?

Instead, she decided that she'd go home, eat every bit of junk food she could find in the house, and wait for him to come home from work. That'd give her time to think things through and come up with the best way to tell him.

She was just about to put the car in drive when she heard a knock on her window. She jumped at the sound but was relieved that it was Andrew again. She pressed the button to roll her window down. "Did I leave something in my office, Andrew?"

Andrew replied, "No ma'am. I just wanted to tell you to be

careful."

Julie thought his statement was odd, but then again, everything about today had been odd. "Thanks, Andrew. Take care."

"You too, Julie."

Andrew's eyes followed Julie's car as it faded into the distance, a dull ache in his chest. He felt a cold breeze on his face as the sky above him turned from blue to gray. He saw the storm clouds gathering, looming over him like a dark threat.

As Julie drove, the silence in the car only fueled her despair, so she cranked up the radio as loud as she could and headed for home.

As she rounded the corner and approached her house, she was shocked to see a silver Mercedes in the driveway. Instantly, she recognized it as Tom's car.

Loud static squelched through the radio and the song changed. A children's chorus began, their voices dark and creepy, *'Use the gun and shoot him dead, shoot him dead, shoot him dead. Use the gun and shoot him dead, my fair lady.'*

Julie's eyes grew wide. "I don't remember hearing that verse before?"

A feeling of dread engulfed her as she pulled into the driveway and turned off the car, extinguishing the haunted voices.

She rushed toward the door, concerned that something was wrong. Tom never took time off from work unless it was an emergency.

Julie set her purse and keys on the table by the door, vaguely noticing that Tom's briefcase was no longer there.

She called out softly, "Tom?"

No answer.

A banging sound issuing from the laundry room greeted

her as she walked inside the living room, sounding like it does when you throw a pair of sneakers into the dryer.

Julie glanced around for a minute and grew even more worried when she couldn't find any sign of Tom. But as she walked into the kitchen toward the laundry room, the banging grew louder and her blood went cold. She pushed the door open a bit and saw through misty eyes that Tom was fucking her sister, Monica, on top of their washing machine! Each thrust was a dagger piercing through her heart.

For a brief second, she thought about throwing the door open and exposing them for their infidelity, but a sinister voice, one that she had never heard before, whispered in her ear. *'Cheaters! Liars! Make them pay! Kill them! Kill them both!'*

A darkness settled over Julie as she softly closed the door, then turned and left the room, moving slowly like a woman possessed, her eyes dark and hollow. The voice whispered to her over and over as she climbed the stairs to the second floor, *'Kill them! Kill them both! Make them pay for their betrayal!'*

A somber and demented look had taken over as she walked down the hallway toward the door at the end. When she walked into the bedroom, she saw Tom's briefcase lying on top of the bed and opened it to reveal an assortment of sexual devices, as well as compromising pictures of Tom and her sister engaged in various sexual activities.

Julie's face was void of all expression as she stood over the bed for a long minute, looking at the contents as if in a trance. There was a definite purpose to her movements when she finally turned and walked toward the closet. The voice in her head became louder, urging her closer to madness. She found the lock-box above her wardrobe, and then the key inside the top drawer of Tom's dresser.

Her hands were eerily steady as Julie sat down on the edge of the bed and inserted the key into the lock. The lid popped open with a click to reveal a loaded handgun inside. As her fingers touched the weapon, the light on the table near the bed flickered for a second.

Her eyes grew darker as she headed back downstairs, the whispers rising to a crescendo in her mind. As she entered the kitchen, Sampson jumped onto the counter and hissed at her warningly. For the briefest of moments, almost imperceptible, she regarded him as Julie. Then the darkness gripped her soul once more.

She approached the laundry room as the screams of passion hit their climax. This time she threw open the door, banging it against the opposite wall and putting a big hole in the plaster.

Tom looked at Julie in horror. Her long black hair hung as a hood around her distraught face, while her mascara had smeared around her eyes, making them look sunken and dead. The countenance of a cold-blooded serial killer gripped her as she pointed the gun at them.

"What in the hell is going on?" she demanded.

Monica's voice was shaky. "It's not what you think, Sis."

It was the classic line that never should be said, but inevitably always was.

Julie's words were full of venom. "So, you weren't just fucking my husband a minute ago? Is that what you're trying to say?"

Monica felt a knot in her throat as she tried to say something, but only a few broken words escaped her lips, conveying no meaningful reply. Instead, she jumped down off the washer and grabbed her clothes off the floor.

Julie snapped at her, "What the fuck are you doing? I didn't say you could move!"

This time Tom spoke up, his lips quivering and his voice cracking, "Listen, Hon. Don't do anything you'll regret."

Julie's eyes pierced through him like frozen daggers. "How could you do this to me? After everything we've gone through? And with my sister no less?"

Her hands gripped the gun a little tighter. "I thought you loved me?"

"I do, dear, believe me."

She knew the words were just a desperate plea from a desperate man trying to save his own ass.

She cocked her head to the side a little in contemplation. She didn't dwell on it long. The icy stare returned quickly. "Well, I don't."

Without hesitation, she pulled the trigger.

The bullet hit Tom squarely in the chest, sending him crashing back into the washing machine. He collapsed in a heap on the laundry room floor, blood spreading quickly over the white ceramic tile.

A scream erupted from Monica before Julie centered the gun on her.

"Shut up," she demanded, as she looked at her sister in disgust. "You always were a little slut, weren't you? That's what they called you in high school—the biggest whore in town. Don't you remember how all the other girls talked about you? Or how all the guys hit on you because you were easy? And who always defended you, huh? And this is how you fucking repay me?"

Monica stammered for something to say, but the only words that came out were, "I'm sorry."

"Me too."

The second bullet struck Monica in the middle of the throat and exited out the back, causing a river of blood to cascade down her chest and onto the floor. She opened her mouth in a dying gasp, sending more blood bubbling down her chin. Her eyes were clouded in disbelief as she slumped to the floor, landing squarely on Tom in a fitting display of their deceit.

Casually, Julie tucked the gun into the back of her pants and walked away. There was one thing left for her to do.

Chapter 11

Michael felt a surge of panic when he found Julie's gun pointed at his face. His forehead was drenched with sweat and his heart pounded in his chest as her eyes regarded him with a ruthless and methodical intent to kill.

"What the fuck are you doing here?" she snapped.

Michael pleaded desperately, "Please don't! You don't know what you're doing. Something's controlling you!"

Julie's face twisted into a demonic abomination. Her mouth grew big and wide, filling her whole face from ear to ear, and when she spoke, rows upon rows of jagged teeth glinted at him, "I know that, you fucking moron!"

Then Julie pulled the trigger. After his body fell to the floor, she straddled over him and emptied the clip, turning his body into Swiss cheese. "I told you to stay out of this!"

Michael heard the door to the laundry room slam shut as he laid there unmoving, paralyzed by both fear and bullet wounds. As everything started to get dark, he thought about Mary and how his death would hurt her yet again. *Maybe it's for the best? She deserves better.* His death would finally set her free to find real happiness.

Failure, however, reared its head again, and he found himself able to move just before the darkness became complete. A series of clanks echoed throughout the laundry room when Michael got up slowly from the floor and the bullets expunged themselves from his flesh.

Michael looked at the twisted naked bodies lying on the floor swimming in blood spilled because of their adultery. "No one deserves to die like that, even if they were cheating bastards," he mumbled.

He saw movement and watched in horror as both figures began twitching. It started at their smallest extremities— fingers and toes wiggling ever-so slightly. He tried to convince himself the movements were just postmortem muscle spasms common among the recently deceased. "That's normal, right?" he mumbled. Then they started to get up.

Their eyes were sunken and dark, like pools of black ink, and a series of unholy growls emanated from their throats. Already, patches of their skin were decaying, causing bits of their flesh to fall to the floor.

He only had a second to react before they sprang forward. Twisting while he grabbed frantically for the door handle, Michael nearly slipped on the sea of blood that now engulfed the floor beneath his feet. Even as he dove through the open door, he felt sharp claws rake across his back.

Desperately, Michael ran through the kitchen toward the doorway on the other side. As he raced into the short hallway on the other side, the angry growls behind him drew closer. Then, dark shadows dancing on the wall ahead of him announced the presence of another group of undead blocking his escape. A doorway to his right provided his only chance at survival.

Michael slammed the door shut and was so surprised to find himself standing in complete darkness on the back porch of an old house, that he nearly fell down the steps. He looked around for a minute, as his eyes adjusted to the night sky.

"This is my old house!" he exclaimed in total shock.

Michael turned back toward the building and heard the angry cries and desperate clawing on the other side of the door. He looked around for an escape, and then stopped, glancing worriedly at the thick forest that lay ominously beyond the backyard. "If this is my old house," he said nervously, "then Grandma's house is through there!"

He walked slowly through the dense brush, careful to stay on the small foot-path that meandered through. The forest was eerily silent and grew darker with each step. The only sound was the soft bubbling of water nearby. A minute later, he stepped out of the trees and stood on the edge of a small stream. Michael looked up to see the silhouette of a small house sitting atop a hill on the other side.

A series of rocks jutted from the water to form a make-shift bridge across the stream. He stepped carefully from one stone to the other, and was almost to the other side when his foot slipped off and he tumbled into the water with a loud splash. As he fell, his face crashed against the side of a rock, creating a long gash across his cheek. "Ow! Fuck!" he exclaimed as he reached his hand to his face and pulled it back covered in blood.

Immediately, the forest came alive with a cacophony of screeches, followed by the beating of wings. Within seconds, an enormous dark shadow crossed the sky, blocking out the moonlight. Then the mass descended toward him.

"Holy shit!" he cried as he scrambled to his feet and scurried to the other side of the stream. He staggered up the steep hill, gasping for air and clutching his aching sides. The deadly flock descended on him savagely, ripping his skin with their talons and beaks. A howl of agony flew from him as he swung his arms desperately to ward off the winged attackers while he dashed the last few yards toward the sanctuary of the house, praying to survive the onslaught.

Michael slammed the door shut just as a flurry of thuds pounded against it, accompanied by a chorus of angry squawks and frantic clawing.

Breathing heavy, with a multitude of cuts and scratches covering him, Michael leaned against the door, trying to catch his breath and calm his nerves. After a minute, he looked around in confusion, trying to understand the madness engulfing him.

Then he saw her in the corner. She was dressed in a pink bathrobe, her hair in curlers, wearing fuzzy house slippers, shuffling back and forth in front of an ironing board draped with a slew of garments. "Grandma?" Michael asked softly.

"She can't hear you," a voice beside him said. "She's deaf as a doornail."

He turned to see a young boy standing there in a stained t-shirt and ripped jeans. His face was covered in dirt and his hair was dotted with sticks, like he'd been playing outside recently. His smile beamed as he looked up at Michael.

"Billy?" Michael asked. "What's going on here?"

"Don't worry 'bout it, Cuz," Billy said. "I got something to show you."

Billy was a few years younger than Michael and had always been a little short of stature. He had a smile so bright and infectious that he could calm the devil himself. He was also dead.

No one knew exactly when he had contracted the terrible disease, a rare form of Tuberculosis called Miliary TB. But when the bacteria infiltrated his bloodstream and quickly spread through his entire body, it shut down multiple organs in a short time, ultimately killing him within two weeks of his diagnosis. The light that he had brought to this world had been extinguished. And through the whole ordeal, with countless friends and family members grieving for such a young soul taken before he had a chance to live, Michael was nowhere to be found.

That's when the darkness creeped in. Every time he closed his eyes, he saw Billy, not the fun-loving kid who had become like a brother, but a weak and shallow boy who lay moments away from Death's door. It was an image he couldn't face, so he ran away.

Michael assumed it was guilt that caused the images to intensify their assault on his mind, but now he knew better. When he saw Billy all those years ago lying on the hospital bed of his dreams—heard his ragged breathing; saw his body stiffen as he took his last breath—it was all very real. He had felt every second of his suffering, and that scared him to death.

After his death, Billy vanished from Michael's dreams completely. Until now. His presence in this particular nightmare brought with it a feeling of foreboding that Michael hadn't felt before. He couldn't begin to fathom where his hellish night-scape would take him next.

Billy reached for the door handle and Michael yelled out desperately, "Wait! You can't go out there!"

Billy looked at him with a hint of disappointment in his eyes. "That's the thing about you, Michael. You always worry about things you don't need to."

Michael was surprised when Billy opened the door to reveal a hallway leading off in both directions.

He followed Billy down the small hallway toward the door that no one in Grandma's house was ever allowed to go—the basement. When Billy started to reach for the handle, Michael stopped him. "You know we're not allowed down there, Billy. Grandma will have our heads if she finds out."

Billy wasn't deterred. "Don't worry about her. She doesn't even know we're here."

Michael thought the statement was odd but didn't stop him further as he twisted the handle and opened the door. A gaping blackness so thick it threatened to suffocate them waited on the other side. Every instinct yelled for Michael to run away, but he was an unwilling participant in this sideshow of horrors and was forced to see it through to the end.

Billy reached up and yanked on a metal chain hanging from a small light fixture in the ceiling. The dim incandescent bulb that flickered to life did little to vanquish the dread. Instead, the rough-hewn stone steps that were illuminated reflected the light in an orange glow that felt like they were about to descend into a secret catacomb where dark spells and animal sacrifices were made by devoted acolytes to appease their ancient gods.

"I don't know about this, Billy?" Michael said in a last-ditch attempt to escape the horror that he knew lurked just around the corner.

Billy ignored his plea and started down the stairs. "Come on," he said over his shoulder after a few steps. "It'll be fun."

As Michael began to descend into the unknown, he touched the stone wall to brace himself, then pulled it back in alarm when he felt something wet and sticky. A cold chill ran through him as he stared at the red substance covering his palm.

"Please tell me this is just paint, Billy?" Michael asked nervously.

Billy chuckled and kept walking.

The deeper they went into the belly of the beast, the thicker the dread became, until Michael could barely breathe. Periodically, Billy would reach up and yank on a chain, bringing another bulb to life. For a brief second, as each light turned on, he heard a brief scuttle and saw shadows wisp away into the darkness ahead.

"We're almost there," Billy said after they had gone much farther than any basement could've contained.

They finally descended into a dimly lit passage that stretched out before them. On either side of the stone walls, iron brackets held candles that cast eerie shadows and revealed arcane symbols carved into the rock. A faint breeze stirred the flames, making them dance and flicker. As they walked, soft voices whispered to them in the dark, as if the passage itself was alive and watching them.

Finally, they came to a small wooden door at the end of the corridor. The rush of musty, stale air that escaped the room beyond as Billy opened the door smelled like old socks that had been soaked in dirty water and left to rot in the sun. "Watch your head," Billy said as he stepped inside.

Michael bent low to enter the room behind Billy. A dim light buzzed and flickered above them, revealing a cramped workshop. A workbench covered with tools and gadgets ran along the far corner of the room. On the wall behind it, hooks held various instruments and devices. On the left, shelves were stacked with jars of nails, screws, bolts, and other hardware. On the right, a sink and a bucket stood next to each other. The bucket was filled with murky water teeming with wriggling worms that smelled like death.

Billy went to the workbench and opened a rusty old toolbox sitting on top. A loud clang echoed through the small room as he set a tray on top of the counter before rummaging through the rest of the contents.

"Where are we, Billy?" Michael asked.

"I'm not sure?" Billy replied without turning around. "I think it might've been Grandpa's. I found it one day when I snuck down here while Grandma was sleeping."

Billy stopped fidgeting with the contents of the chest for a moment and his shoulders dropped. "Why didn't you come and see me, Michael?" he said softly.

The question hit Michael hard. It was the same one he had tormented himself with over and over. What was he supposed to say? That he was scared? That he was a coward? The only thing he could find himself saying was, "I'm sorry."

Billy still wouldn't face him. "I get it," he said. "It was a hard time. For everyone. But you were like a big brother to me. I looked up to you and I needed you there with me."

Tears streamed down Michael's face as he thought about the moment he found out Billy was going to die. "I wanted to see you. Really, I did. But I also wanted to remember you the way you always were to me—happy and carefree. I was afraid if I saw you in the hospital, I would lose that."

"So, you didn't come and visit me on my death-bed because you were being selfish?"

Billy was silent for a second before he went back to rifling through the toolbox.

"I worshiped you, Michael," he continued after a minute. "You were my idol. I tried everything to be like you. I dressed like you. I talked like you. I even ate the same food as you. But I always felt like I came up short. Now, I think I've figured it out."

When Billy finally spun around, Michael stood paralyzed with a look of shock plastered on his face. A dozen syringes jutted from Billy's arms, each one filled with a different color liquid. White powder crusted the top of his upper lip and tip of his nose. His eyes were wide and bloodshot, like a crazed animal. Sweat poured down his forehead, making his skin glisten. And as he started to speak, small trickles of white foam bubbled from his mouth. "What do you think?" he asked excitedly. "Am I doing it right?"

Michael tried to scream, but nothing came out.

Billy yanked a needle out of his arm and walked up to Michael, "Your turn. You're the pro, after all. Why don't you show me how it's really done?"

Michael watched helplessly as Billy reared back and plunged the tip of the needle into his chest.

Billy took a step back and looked at Michael like an artist criticizing his own work. After a minute, he said, "Looks like you're losing your touch, Michael. I think you're gonna need a little more juice to really get this trip going!"

He pulled the remaining needles from his body and plunged them into Michael's body, arranging them in the shape of a heart covering his torso. He chuckled, "See, I'm not completely heartless."

Billy held his arms out to his side to relish in the moment. Then, a chorus of scuttling closed in, as a legion of insects invaded the room. The creatures climbed onto Billy, covering him until he became a writhing mass of insects. His form grew taller until it reached the ceiling.

For a moment, the insects scurried away from Billy's face to reveal Belial looking down at Michael. "You really don't get it, do you, you insufferable fuck? I don't care who you are, you are not going to interfere with my plan!"

The writhing mass opened its mouth wide and bent down, snapping Michael up and swallowing him whole.

Chapter 12

Julie walked back toward the front door, her eyes still full of rage, snatched her keys off the stand, and walked out to her car. She left the front door wide open, but that didn't matter. She knew she wouldn't be coming back.

As Julie walked toward her car, she ran her key along the side of Tom's car in a last act of defiance. She didn't see the black shadowy mass that followed her out of the house and into the car, filling the back seat with its writhing form.

Julie turned on the car and cranked up the radio. The speakers screeched and the children start singing again. This time, Julie turned the volume up louder. *'Take the ax and chop him up, chop him up, chop him up. Take the ax and chop him up, my fair lady.'*

Without so much as a glance toward her house, she backed out of the driveway and raced away. Nothing in the world seemed to matter anymore. The only thing on her mind was to finish what she started. No matter what.

This time, she made it to the agency without incident. The parking lot was a ghost town when she pulled in, her tires coming to a screeching halt against the curb. As she reached for the door handle, the dark mass enveloped her for a second before dissipating. Her eyes clouded over briefly before returning to normal.

Andrew was the ever-vigilant watchman at the front entrance, reminding Julie of the boatman waiting to take the lost souls across the river Styx. She thought she saw a tear glistening down his cheek, almost as if he knew what was about to happen. *How could he? I don't even know exactly what's going to happen.*

"Can I help you with something, Ma'am?" Andrew said as Julie approached the door.

"I just forgot something, Andrew. It'll only take a minute."

"You know I'm not supposed to let you back in the building."

She pleaded with him, "I know, Andrew. But it won't take long, and nobody will even know I'm here. I promise." That was a lie. It would probably take a long time and everyone in the building would know about it.

Andrew finally conceded. As she walked past him, she had the distinct feeling that he was trying to stall her long enough so that she might change her mind. But she had already passed the point of no return.

"Goodbye, Mrs. Dunbar," he said as she walked into the lobby.

Those three words hit her like a sledgehammer. Julie realized for the first time the magnitude of her crime. She had murdered the two people in her life that had ever mattered to her; shot them in cold blood. It didn't matter that they had betrayed her love and her trust. No one deserved to die in such a way. For the first time, she felt sorry for what she had done. Unfortunately, there was no turning back now. She had chosen her path. Now she had to see it through to the end.

She walked quickly past Tammy at the reception desk to avoid any kind of interaction. She almost made it to the elevator, but then Tammy spoke up, "Don't worry, Hon, everything will be alright. It always is in the end. Just be strong and know what you have to do."

Julie stopped. Darkness instantly clouded her eyes as the whispers in her mind spoke up once more. *Kill them! Kill them all!*

Without hesitation, she whipped the gun out and spun around. "You know, Tammy, that's the most helpful thing you've ever said to me!"

Then she pulled the trigger. A trail of blood marked the spot where Tammy's head had hit the wall before her body slumped to the floor.

The elevator door opened and the chamber inside beckoned to her with its dark whisper. The door closed loudly as she entered, sounding like a jail cell slamming shut behind her. Indeed, she knew now she was nothing more than a dead woman walking.

Julie exited the elevator a minute later and proceeded toward her old office. The few employees there didn't seem to notice her.

She glanced down at the end of the hall and saw Mr. Price's silhouette behind the smoked glass in his office. Quietly, she entered her office and closed the door.

For a moment, Julie's senses returned, and she felt the full magnitude of the atrocities she had committed. *My god, what have I done? I don't know if I can go through with this?*

She heard a deep laugh echo through the office. "It's too late to stop now!" it hissed.

When she spun around, each wall had been transformed into a gigantic movie screen. The scene was the same on each one: Tom thrusting himself hard into her sister while she urged him on, with a slew of obscenities pouring from her mouth. She heard the same pounding on the washing machine; the same passionate lovemaking sounds; saw the same sweat running down their bodies.

Then the scene shifted to Mr. Price, the one who had started her spiral into Hell. His face beamed with joy as he said those two words that had set her off on her present course: "You're fired!"

Julie spun around, holding her hands over her ears and closing her eyes to try to escape the onslaught. But the scene kept playing itself over and over in an evil, twisted loop, and finally, she couldn't take it anymore. A loud scream erupted from her with enough force to vanquish the chaos surrounding her. But the madness in her mind had grown unstoppable. It scratched and clawed at her brain, whispering incessantly, *You know what you have to do...There's no turning back now...It's all his fault...He deserves everything he gets.*

Whipping the gun from the small of her back, Julie threw open her office door and marched down the hallway with the crazed look of a lunatic plastered on her face, ignoring the cries and screams that now filled the air.

When a young intern, whose name she couldn't remember, suddenly appeared before her, oblivious to the shrieks of her fellow associates, Julie was wound so tight that she couldn't stop from pulling the trigger and putting a bullet in her chest. The girl slumped to the floor amid a shower of documents she'd been carrying.

For a second, as the blood turned the white pages red, Julie felt a hint of remorse. Then Mr. Price stuck his head out of his office to see the source of the commotion, prompting the madness to take over once again. She stepped over the twitching body and marched down the hall, the voice in her head shouting, *Kill him! Kill him! Kill him!*

The large man stumbled back into his office and desperately slammed the door shut, locked it behind him.

A fire extinguisher and axe beckoned to Julie from an emergency case on the wall nearby. She whipped her gun around and shot the glass before wrenching the axe from its perch. With the strength of the darkness inside her, she violently attacked the heavy door, chopping it to pieces quickly.

Julie stepped through the opening carrying the axe in her left hand and holding the gun in her right. Mr. Price backed up further into the room, tripping over his chair, and falling to the floor. His body trembled as Julie puts the barrel of the gun against his forehead.

"Please, Julie, you don't have to do this," he said, on the verge of hysteria.

Julie looked at him fiercely. "Do you have any idea how much pain you caused me, you inconsiderate fuck? You ruined my whole life when you fired me!"

"Look...I was only doing my job. I'm sorry. You left me with no choice."

Julie cocked her head to one side and looked at him for a second. "Same here."

She pulled the trigger, sending the bullet exiting through the back of his head and causing a spray of brains and blood to cover the office floor.

'Take the ax and chop him up, chop him up, chop him up. Take the ax and chop him up, my fair lady.'

Julie put the gun on his desk and raised the axe up high. "It didn't have to be this way, Mr. Price. All you had to do was give me another chance. But, no, you had to be a stickler for the rules, didn't you?"

She brought the axe down hard, severing through his neck. Then she repeated the act until his body lay in countless bloody pieces on the floor. She dropped the axe next to the mangled remains and retrieved the gun, looking at the bloody mess for a moment. "Well, that's gross!"

No one popped out at her unexpectedly on her way back to her former office, saving her from killing another intern accidentally. Once inside, she tossed the gun on the desk and stood there for a minute, deciding on her next move.

Julie's eyes shifted from the weapon to the window and back again. She pointed her finger back and forth. "Eenie, meenie, minie, die. Shoot the bastard in the eye. Eenie, meenie, minie, more. Shoot the bimbo, shoot the whore."

Her finger stopped on the window.

With a steady hand, she aimed the gun at the window and squeezed the trigger. A second later, the glass exploded, sending shards flying in all directions. Julie glanced out at the darkening sky that had turned from gray to black, and felt a surge of adrenaline as she stepped out onto the thin ledge that wrapped around the building. Instantly, a jolt of fear hit her. But what made her heart stop wasn't the extreme height but the sight of another person standing there!

"Good afternoon, Julie," Belial said. "I've been expecting you."

Julie almost lost her balance until Belial reached out and caught hold of her.

"Whoa!" he said. "We can't have you falling prematurely. That would kind of defeat the purpose, don't you think?"

She stared at Belial in shock for a minute. "Who are you? And what are you doing out here?"

"Who I am doesn't matter as much as why I'm here?" Belial replied.

"Which is?"

"Consider me your counselor in this time of need."

Julie was lost in an endless sea of confusion. "How did you

know I'd be out here?"

"I know lots of things, Julie. I know that you're hurting like you've never hurt before; that you feel betrayed. And I'm here to help you get through this difficult time."

Julie started crying a deep and mournful cry that erupted from the depths of her soul. "What do I do now? I didn't want to kill them, but I lost control. Before I knew it, they were all dead. All I ever wanted was to be loved."

Belial looked at her quietly for a moment, then said, "I'd say you're in a pretty sticky situation, Julie. After all, you did just brutally murder your husband and sister. Then you followed that up with a bullet to your boss's brain. Not to mention, the intern who was in the wrong place at the wrong time. And lastly, the receptionist, although she had it coming to her. I'm afraid there's no coming back from all that."

Julie's head slunk low, and she watched through misty eyes as the world rolled by down below, unaware of her tribulation.

"I think you know there's only one thing left to do." Belial said.

The whispers rose again in Julie's ear, chanting a chorus. Her head started spinning. "I don't know if I can go through with this," she sobbed. "I'm so scared."

Belial wrapped his arm around her shoulder to encourage her. "You can do this, Julie. You're stronger than you think. I assure you it'll happen so fast you won't feel a thing."

The children's voices filled her ears once more, *'Tear it down with blood and guts, blood and guts, blood and guts. Tear it down with blood and guts, my fair lady.'*

A baby's cry drifted up to her from far below. She looked over the edge and saw a blue stroller on the sidewalk at the foot of the building beckoning to her.

"He's waiting for you." Belial said.

Julie looked at Belial for a second, and then back down, before she closed her eyes and took a deep breath.

***

Michael was standing on a small ledge outside a large office building. The demon from the office was standing next to him, dressed in a suit and tie, with the woman beside him.

Belial looked at Michael and yelled, "What the fuck are you doing here? Haven't you had enough? No one invited you!"

Then he calmed himself down, running his hands over his hair, brushing dust from the arms of his suit, straightening his tie. "It doesn't matter, though. You're too late."

Michael watched in horror as the woman closed her eyes and leaped from the ledge. She fell like a stone, her body twisting and turning in the air. He wanted to scream, to do something, but he was frozen with fear. He could only watch as the woman hit the ground with a sickening thud.

A second later, Michael felt himself falling too. He closed his eyes and braced for impact. The ground rushed up to meet him, and his body slammed into the pavement. As his bones broke and his flesh tore, silently, he screamed out.

Chapter 13

A violent jolt ripped Michael out of his nightmare and he crashed onto the living room floor. His lungs felt like they were burning as he gasped for air, clutching his chest. He crawled to the couch and leaned against it, shaking uncontrollably.

Once he had calmed down, he stood up and shuffled to the kitchen. After moving a few boxes around, he found the prize he had hidden in the back of the bottom shelf.

Michael held the bottle tight against his chest like a newborn baby. A brief feeling of guilt passed through him as he unscrewed the cap and took a big swig. He closed his eyes as he swallowed hard, letting the fiery liquid calm his nerves.

He almost dropped the bottle when he heard Mary's voice behind him. "What the fuck do you think you're doing?!"

Michael turned around and saw her standing there with fury burning in her eyes. "Mary? What are you doing here?"

Mary replied, "I came to check on your sorry ass. It's a good thing I came by when I did!"

"I just needed something to calm me down," Michael

sputtered. "I'm sorry."

"You told me you'd gotten clean! That you hadn't been drinking or using for months!"

"I was clean," he pleaded. "You gotta believe me. But the nightmares started again and I couldn't take it."

"You lied to me, you piece of shit!"

As a wave of guilt-ridden tears overcame him, Michael tried to reach out for her but she swatted his hand away.

"You're so pathetic, Michael. A couple of bad dreams and you run for the first thing you can, and then you're right back on the wagon. It's always been the quick and easy way out for you, hasn't it?"

"I'm sorry, Mary. I'll get rid of it right now."

He walked over to the kitchen sink and was about to pour the contents of the bottle down the drain, but Mary stopped him.

"I have a better idea," she said.

Mary grabbed the bottle in one hand and Michael's wrist in the other. She clamped her fingers around his arm with a force that made him wince. Dragging him back into the living room, she flung him onto the recliner like a rag-doll.

When he tried to get up, a set of restraints burst through the arms and feet of the chair and clamped onto his wrists and ankles, holding him tight.

"I think it's time to try a fresh approach," Mary said as she tilted the recliner back as far as it would go.

"When I was a little girl, there was a time I gorged myself on Reece's Peanut Butter Cups. I found a bag of them stashed in the cupboard and ate every single one of them before my mom got home. I thought I was so clever until I got sick later and puked my guts out. To this day, I can't stand the sight or smell of them."

She held the bottle above Michael's face. "Let's see if this will have the same effect. Although, there's a chance that you'll either drown or die from alcohol poisoning, in which case it won't matter, anyway."

With her free hand, she grabbed his nose and pinched it shut. He tried to shake his head free of her grasp, but she was too strong. Finally, he had no choice but to open his mouth and gasp for air. When he tried to breathe again, she tipped the bottle and poured the liquid down his throat. The liquor burned his esophagus as he gagged and sputtered.

Mary laughed while he struggled to stay alive. "How does that taste, you bastard? Had enough yet?"

Then her face changed and Belial leaned close to him, "This is your last warning, boy! Stay out of this, or you'll be sorry!"

Michael felt the last bit of oxygen escape his lungs as he fell under the power of the demon.

***

Liquid mixed with bile flew from Michael's mouth as he fell to the floor, coughing and gagging. He looked around in a panic to find that he was back in his living room. When the coughing turned to retching, and he vomited onto the floor, he smelled the unmistakable scent of alcohol.

He fumbled in his pocket and pulled out his phone, searching with trembling fingers for Mary's number. When she answered, the only thing he could mutter was, "I need you."

When Mary raced through the door minutes later, the stench of vomit and alcohol hit her immediately. That didn't matter as much as the visage of the tortured man sitting in front of her. His eyes held a darkness in them she had never seen before.

He looked at her weakly as she walked toward him and cried. "I don't know what's going on with me, Mary. I feel like I'm falling apart. I'm so scared."

The only thing that Mary could do was hold him tight. "It'll be okay," she said as she laid her head against his and caressed the hair away from his brow.

After a while, the fear and trembling subsided, and Michael looked into Mary's eyes. "I'm losing it, Mary, and I don't know what to do. These nightmares seem so real. It doesn't make any sense."

"I think we need to get you some professional help."

"What kind of help?" Michael asked skeptically.

"There's a section at the hospital for people with mental disorders—"

"You mean the psycho ward? That's just great! Even you think I'm fucking crazy."

"If you'd let me finish; I was going to say that they also help people with sleep disorders. They treat people for things like insomnia, sleepwalking, night terrors. They might be able to figure something out?"

Michael calmed down a little. He hadn't thought of sleep therapy. It might help? He also knew he couldn't face this evil alone. "Okay, you win. Make the appointment," he said.

"Michael, it's not a matter of winning or losing. It's a matter of helping you deal with whatever's going on."

Mary pulled out her phone and made a call. After talking for a minute, she hung up and looked at Michael with a surprised look on her face.

"Let me guess, they told you to fuck off?" Michael said.

Mary shook her head. "Well, that was unexpected."

"What was?"

"We have an appointment this afternoon."

"That's fast! I figured it'd take a couple weeks to get in."

"The doctor sounded very eager to help."

"I'm sure they did," Michael mumbled.

***

They arrived at the hospital a few minutes before three. Michael took a seat on a chair near the front desk, while Mary walked up to the counter, where a receptionist sat behind a counter with an array of computer monitors arranged near her.

"We have an appointment for three o'clock," Mary said.

"Name?" the woman replied stiffly.

"Michael Sanders."

The receptionist peered over the desk at Michael, who was sulking in his chair, and smiled. She typed on her keyboard for a second and then picked up the phone. "Sir, he's here," she said to the entity on the other end of the line.

Her eyes darted toward Michael once more. "Yes, sir...of course."

The receptionist hung up the phone and turned toward Mary. "The doctor is finishing with another patient at the moment and will be out shortly."

Mary nodded and joined Michael in the small waiting area. "How are you holding up?" she asked as she sat down next to him.

Michael shrugged, "Okay, I guess. About as good as I can be."

"Just hang in there. This'll all be over soon."

Michael was about to reply when a tall man with gray, bushy hair and dark-rimmed glasses, looking like a modern-day Einstein, rushed out to meet them. Small splatters of blood dotted the front of his white lab coat.

Michael reluctantly rose from his chair, eyeing the doctor

warily.

The doctor extended his arm and shook Michael's hand eagerly as if he was meeting a celebrity whom he had idolized since childhood. "Welcome, Michael! We're excited that we could see you on such short notice!"

He turned toward Mary. "And you must be Mary? Thank you for calling. I'm Dr. Belhorn. Please, follow me! We're eager to get started."

As Dr. Belhorn led them from the waiting area, Michael glanced toward the receptionist, who had a lunatic smile plastered on her face and was waving excitedly.

The doctor led them down a short, dimly lit hallway toward an elevator. Michael's skin crawled, as a series of faint screeches, like nails on a chalkboard, sounded in the distance.

Dr. Belhorn smiled at Michael as he pressed the button to call the elevator. "This is going to be so much fun! I can feel it," he said enthusiastically.

"I wouldn't call what I'm dealing with fun.," Michael said.

"It's all just a matter of perspective, Michael. When one embraces the chaos, magical things can happen."

Before Michael could respond, the elevator doors opened, and the doctor ushered them inside. He whistled a happy tune as he pressed the solitary button on the panel that began a slow descent into the unknown.

Bizarre music blasted from the speaker in the ceiling, a mixture of metal and nursery rhymes, with a haunting voice belting out a deluge of freakish words: *'Great green gobs of greasy grimy girly guts.'*

Dr. Belhorn exclaimed, "Ooh, I haven't heard this one in a long time!"

Then he started singing along, "Flappy flippy flirty feet, juicy mangled maiden meat."

Mary joined him. "Great big bunches of eyeballs rolling

down the street, but I didn't forget my spoon."

Michael looked at her shocked.

"What?" Mary replied. "It's a rhyme my Nanna used to sing to me."

"You know those lyrics are really fucked up, right?" Michael said.

Mary chuckled. "I'm just trying to lighten up a little. You should try it. It might help you deal with your shit.

"She's right," Dr. Belhorn said. "When you resist something, it only brings it to you with greater force."

Finally, the elevator came to a stop, and the doors opened.

Dr. Belhorn led them from the elevator, walking at a quick pace like a man on a mission, through a series of twists and turns until they were in a long hallway. A crimson hue coated the walls, creating a stark contrast with the unsettling artworks that hung haphazardly on them. The paintings depicted twisted shapes and forms that defied any logic or harmony.

Finally, they came to a door at the end of the hallway with the word 'Bedlam' posted above. Michael didn't know what that word meant, but he didn't like the sound of it.

The doctor stopped and pushed the door open, gesturing for Michael and Mary to go in first. "After you," he said politely.

After walking into the room, the door clicked behind them, and Michael felt a surge of fear. He barely had time to turn his head when powerful claws seized his arms, pinning him in place. He stared in horror at the green-scaled beasts that towered over him, their lizard-like eyes gleaming with malice. Mary whirled around and met his gaze, her eyes flashing dangerously. "Why do you keep trying to interfere, Michael? Don't you see it's useless to fight?"

The doctor stepped to Mary's side, and his face changed to

Belial's. "It's time to end this struggle, Michael," he said.

The scaly horrors dragged Michael to a sinister table in the corner of the room. He thrashed and fought as they secured his limbs to the iron rails with tight straps. They fitted a metal helmet over his head, linking it to a web of wires and electrodes. He felt a surge of pain and panic as sharp needles pricked his scalp, unleashing waves of torment through his mind.

Mary stepped over to a console a short distance from Michael's imprisonment. "It's for your own good, Michael," she said. "Now, try to relax. This will only hurt a lot!"

Then she flipped a switch that sent a surge of electricity into his brain. Michael's body twitched violently back and forth on the table as the energy wracked through him. Blood and mucous flew from his mouth and nose, splattering the wall beside him and cascading down his shirt onto the floor. The pain lasted an eternity it seemed, before he finally passed out.

***

When Michael finally regained consciousness, he was relieved to find he was back in his apartment, free from the demons that had tortured his dreams, but he was also disappointed to see that he was alone. After a quick check around, Mary was nowhere to be found.

He wiped his eyes on the sleeve of his shirt and shuffled toward the pantry in the kitchen. He rummaged around for a bit and found the bottle of vodka hidden in the bottom. His fingers tingled as he grabbed it, sending a shock-wave of deja vu running through his brain. In rapid succession, he saw the hatred in Mary's eyes, felt the strength of her grip as she slammed him into the chair, and then the helplessness as he gasped for air while drowning in the waterfall of alcohol at her hands.

With a trembling hand, he put the bottle on the kitchen counter, vowing to never touch the stuff again.

***

The room inside was part television studio and part Dr. Frankenstein's lab. Sparks of electricity crackled overhead from a series of wires that ran from a bank of monitors that covered one wall, snaked across the ceiling, and converged together in the far corner of the room. The pigtail was plugged into a cable attached to the back of a large iron chair. The chair was occupied by a naked young woman strapped to it with thick restraints—Elizabeth Bathory. She had a ball-gag in her mouth, and a metal helm on her head covered with electrodes.

Belial sat at the desk, watching the array of monitors in front of him. Fluorescent lights flickered on the ceiling above him, giving off an eerie glow. Outside the room, he could hear the tortured screams of his children echoing through the halls of the asylum. He leaned forward in his chair to study the screen closer, showing Michael on the floor of his apartment, crying.

Although the sight of him curled up in a fetal position sent a smile across his lips, his presence during Julie's manipulation was cause for concern. He reached forward and pressed a button on the desk. "Nazur? Can you come in here, please?"

Seconds later, a tall, lanky man with a bulbous head and long nose entered the room carrying a clipboard in his hand. "Yes, My Lord?"

"I want a full report as soon as possible about this little

piss-ant here that's been interfering," Belial said as he pointed to the screen. "Find out everything you can about him. Torture whoever you have to. Just get me what I need. I have a feeling he's going to be a nuisance. And I can't afford any distractions.

"Right away, My Lord!", Nazur said as he jotted a couple of notes down and exited the room, leaving Belial visibly irritated as he continued to study Michael's image on the screen.

Finally, Belial got up from his chair and crossed to the other side of the room where four images were tacked up horizontally on a bulletin board-three males and one female —like wanted posters once found plastered on post office walls. The first picture in the row was Julie's. He yanked the picture off the board and looked at it for a second as if appreciating a piece of art he'd created.

"One down. Three to go," he said before the picture burst into flames and turned to ash in his hand.

Belial returned to his desk and looked at the bank of monitors before him, reveling in the torment he had unleashed.

Chapter 14

When the alarm started blaring, Harold quickly reached over and turned it off. He slowly turned over and was relieved to see that Sharon was still snoring softly. His relief soon grew into disgust when he took in the full picture of her laying sprawled out, leaving all of her folds and wrinkles bare in a display that nearly burned his eyes. He shook his head before he got up and shambled into the bathroom, his own belly protruding from under his t-shirt.

After a quick shower, he quietly dressed for work and left the room, careful not to wake the beast.

He slung his tie around his neck and tied it loosely before he grabbed his briefcase on the way to the door. He was inches away from freedom when her voice stopped him. "Were you leaving without saying goodbye?"

Harold rolled his eyes and turned around to see Sharon standing there wearing a blue bathrobe and a severe case of bed head. For a moment, he felt like a caged animal. "Sorry. You were asleep when I got up and I didn't want to wake you."

Sharon frowned as she walked up and straightened his tie. "Well, try to have a good day at work, okay?"

Harold answered her with a grunt and gave her a brief peck of a kiss on the cheek before turning back toward the door.

"Don't forget I have a meeting this afternoon that might run late," he said as he grabbed the door handle. "I'll be home as soon as I can."

The tires squealed just a little as Harold pulled out of the driveway and stepped on the gas, eager to get away.

Harold had no delusions about his work at Franklin and Sons Insurance, LLC. It was a monotonous routine that left him feeling bored and unfulfilled. How could anyone make insurance interesting? Yet he was good at it and it paid the bills. But lately, he felt like he was in a slump and his performance was declining.

He leaned on his desk in front of his computer display, talking to a client through his headset. His voice sounded annoyed and impatient as he finished the conversation. "Thank you, sir. Have a good day."

He ripped his headpiece off and tossed it on the desk in frustration.

A second later, Jeremy, a tall man in his thirties, peeked over the top of his cubicle from the front, frowning. "That didn't sound like it went so well."

"Yeah, not quite," Harold replied bitterly. "I'm trying to close the Haffner deal, but the guy's a dick."

Jeremy snorted, "Don't I know it? I've had to deal with him before. Strung me along for months before he finally committed. His son is even a bigger dick than he is."

"Thanks for warning me. If he calls, I'll forward *him to you.*"

Jeremy chuckled. "Hey, I'm having a barbecue this weekend.

Why don't you bring Sharon and the kids?"

Harold shook his head. "Sorry, Sharon has a couple of projects she wants me to work on."

"Can't that wait until next week?"

"She's been on my ass forever. If I wanna shut her up, I need to get this done."

Jeremy shrugged, "Okay, suit yourself. The invitation's still open if you change your mind."

Harold replied with a stiff nod, and Jeremy slunk back into his cubicle.

The rest of the morning was equally ineffective. Call after call resulted in rejection, and Harold figured his day was more than likely going to end the same way it began: in disappointment. Everything seemed a disappointment these days. *Sounds about right,* Harold thought bitterly. His job was a disappointment. His family was a disappointment. Hell, even he was a disappointment.

After finally making a small sale, a tiny life insurance policy for an elderly man, he decided the rest of the day would be spent aimlessly surfing the Internet rather than pursuing other clients. *Better to quit while you're ahead.*

When Jeremy suddenly popped his head up again, it startled Harold. He hadn't realized how much he'd lost track of time. He glanced up to see that the clock on the wall read four forty-five.

"Me and Tom are gonna head to the bar after work for a drink. You wanna join?" Jeremy asked.

"No, I have some things to finish up here," Harold lied. He wasn't in the mood to socialize. Wasn't really in the mood for anything.

"Hey, man, you're bringing me down," Jeremy laughed, trying to lighten Harold's mood. "You need to liven up a bit!"

Yeah, tell me about it, Harold thought as he watched Jeremy grab his jacket and leave the office. *If only it were that easy.*

A few minutes later, Harold was the only one left in the office. The silence was eerie, almost unsettling, but he shrugged it off and resumed his web surfing. He stumbled onto a dating site called Sweet Temptations that caught his eye. He clicked on the link and started browsing through different profiles until a voice behind him caused him to jump. "Lookin' for a date?"

Harold turned around to see a middle-aged black male wearing a janitor uniform standing there holding the handle of a mop while the head of it rested halfway in and halfway out of the bucket, dripping dirty water on the floor at his feet.

"Oh...uh...no, just browsing a little," Harold replied as his face flushed.

"Well, if you were, that's a damn good site."

"And you are?"

The man let the mop handle drop to the floor and quickly wiped his hand on his pant leg before extending it to Harold, "Sorry. The name's Benny. Just started here a couple days ago."

Harold accepted the man's hand hesitantly, "You've used this site before?"

Benny smiled proudly. "A couple times. Got me a fine little piece of ass out of it."

Harold held up his hands defensively. "I was just curious, that's all. I'm actually happily married."

Benny looked at Harold for a second and smiled. "I didn't mean nothing by it. What you do on your own time is your business. Maybe, though, you're not as happy as you thought?"

Harold's face grew defiant, "You don't even know me! How would you know if I'm happy or not?"

Benny remained cool, "If you were, you wouldn't be

looking at shit like that."

When he saw Harold get agitated, he said, "Listen, man, don't get upset. I've been in your shoes—a dead-end relationship where all the passion and romance have dried up like an old lady's snatch. How is a man supposed to be happy like that?"

Harold calmed down a little and asked, "What did you do?"

Benny replied, "Found me a little side piece to fill the gap, or rather whose gap I filled, if you know what I mean."

"But I could never cheat on my wife!"

"It's only cheating if you get caught," Benny said as he winked at Harold before he walked away.

***

Michael stood in the corner as Benny walked toward him. Harold didn't seem to notice Michael as he shuffled out of the office.

"Well, well, this is a surprise!" Benny said as he looked Michael up and down a couple of times, studying him. "Shit's about to get really interesting up in here!"

Benny whistled a cheerful tune as he walked away, leaving Michael stunned.

Chapter 15

Harold trudged toward his car, thinking about the strange encounter with the strange man. He was surprised to find a business flyer tucked under the windshield wiper for the same dating site he saw on his computer. The whole encounter was getting stranger by the second. He thought about crumpling it up, determined to put the whole incident to rest, but something stopped him and instead he folded it up and put it in his pocket.

As Harold drove through town, the radio mocked him with love song after love song on every station. He was just about to change the channel again when the song ended and an ad for Sweet Temptations came on. *Now I know the universe is fucking with me!* He sighed and turned the radio off.

After pulling into his driveway, Harold reached for the door handle and then hesitated, sitting in the car for a minute in contemplation. He knew what to expect and took a deep breath to prepare himself. He thought briefly of running away; finding somewhere to hide. Maybe he could call Sharon and tell her he had to work later than expected? Or that traffic was bad, and he didn't know what time he'd be home? At least that would delay the torture. A long sigh drew out of him. He was already home and any thought of escape was futile. He finally resigned himself to his fate and walked up to the front door.

As he prepared himself to face the inevitable, he picked at a speck of paint that was chipping away from the door-frame and immediately wished he hadn't. "Shit!" he grumbled. "Now she'll probably want me to paint the whole fucking house!"

He sighed as he turned the handle, praying silently that today would be different. He should've known better.

He immediately heard the screams and yells coming from his teenage sons fighting, followed by the bellow of Sharon's voice telling them to stop. Mingled in with the uproar was their daughter, Casey's cry. The distinctly charred smell that caught his nose as he walked in told him Sharon had been trying to cook again. *Welcome home, Harold Wagner,* he thought bitterly.

He shouted a little louder than usual, just to make sure everyone heard him. "Honey, I'm home!"

"Thank god!" Sharon cried as she rounded the corner from the kitchen. "Can you shut those boys of yours up for a minute? They're about to drive me nuts."

Harold dropped his eyes and whispered under his breath, "Happy to see you too, dear."

He proceeded toward the family room where he found his youngest son, David, trussed in a headlock by his oldest son, Jared. Howls of pain issued from him as Jared refused to let go. In the room's corner, little Casey sat in her playpen, crying amidst the chaos.

"Ok, the two of you, stop it now!" Harold bellowed.

Jared looked at his dad with sweat dripping down his

forehead. "But he started it!"

"I did not!" David replied through clenched teeth.

"I don't care who started it! I said stop! Now!"

Reluctantly, Jared loosened his grip on David's head.

David spun away and tried to catch his breath, but just when it looked like the melee had ended, he drew back and sucker-punched Jared in the back of the head.

Jared whirled around quickly; his fist ready to come crashing down.

Harold snatched both boys' arms and held them firmly apart, glaring at them. "I am not in the mood for this shit tonight! If you don't straighten up right now, you'll be sorry. Do you understand?"

Both boys looked at their dad fearfully. In unison, they responded, "Yes."

"Good! Now go to your rooms until dinner's ready."

The slamming doors upstairs a minute later told Harold they weren't exactly happy. *Oh well.*

"You've got to do something, Harold," Sharon said once the boys had left. "They're getting out of control!"

"Why am I the one that needs to do something?" Harold asked, "You could help me out a little bit here."

"Don't go putting this on me. I'm trying my best here. You know they don't listen to me."

"Sorry, I didn't mean it that way. I just meant that with me at work all day, I can't be here to act as referee. What were they fighting about?"

"Who knows? Same shit, different day."

"I'll talk to them later," Harold said before he got up and headed upstairs.

***

As Harold was changing out of his work clothes, he felt the folded paper buried in his pants pocket. He peered around the room to make sure Sharon hadn't followed him upstairs before he pulled the flyer out and unfolded it. He gazed at the ad longingly for a moment before he crumpled it up and threw it in the trash can beside the nightstand like he had done with the rest of his dreams.

He let out a long and heavy sigh, feeling the weight of his exhaustion and frustration. He dragged himself to his closet and grabbed the first clothes he could find: a pair of worn-out sweatpants and a faded t-shirt. He pulled them on with little care and trudged back downstairs, dreading what awaited him. On his way down, he asked the boys to join him for a terse conversation.

Both sat nervously on opposite ends of the couch as Harold sat in the chair across from them with a stern look on his face.

"Now, what was that crap all about when I came home?" Harold demanded.

Neither of the boys answered.

Harold persisted, "If someone doesn't answer, I'm really going to get pissed!"

Jared finally spoke up, "He took my skateboard without asking!"

"Only because you broke mine!" David answered.

"I did not!" Jared said.

"Yes, you did! How else could it have broken?"

"Maybe it was from your fat ass riding on it?"

David jumped from the couch with his fist clenched. Harold quickly grabbed him before another brawl ensued. "I've had enough of this shit! Both of you are grounded for two weeks. No friends, no TV, and certainly no skateboards!"

Cries and pleas flew from the boys' mouths.

"We can make it three weeks if you'd like?" Harold warned.

Both boys shook their heads sadly.

Harold eyed them both. "Good. Now, grow up, both of you!"

Sharon peeked her head into the room and said meekly, "Dinner's ready."

The boys slowly got up from the couch and shuffled out of the room, with Harold following close behind.

A chill hung in the air as the family sat around the dinner table, barely touching their food. No one dared to speak or make eye contact. Even little Casey, who usually chattered away, sensed the tension and clamped her mouth shut. It was as if they were a family of death-row inmates eating their last meals.

***

Michael watched sadly from the foot of the table as the broken family ate their meal in silence. Sadness quickly turned to horror when Harold's eyes started bleeding. He looked around the table and saw that all of them were experiencing the same assault. A squishy sound brought his gaze to the maggots that squirmed through the rotted food on their plates.

He tried to back away from the table, but was slammed down into a chair opposite Harold, as vines rose from the floor and grabbed his arms. A silver-covered dish sat on the table before him.

"Why don't you join us for dinner?" Harold said with an evil grin. "I insist!"

Like a proud chef, Sharon added, "I made this dish just for you! I'm sure you're gonna love it!"

A scream flew from Michael's mouth when Sharon removed the dome, revealing Mary's severed head lying amidst a bed of greens. Her haunted eyes pleaded with him as her pale mouth twitched open and closed.

***

Harold finally had a few minutes of peace to himself. Sharon was putting Casey to bed, and the boys had decided to seclude themselves in their rooms for the rest of the night. He plopped down in his chair with a beer in one hand and the remote in the other. His solitude was interrupted a few minutes later when Sharon joined him. He grumbled and took a swig of his beer before he changed the channel.

"What do you want to watch?" he asked with a hint of irritation in his voice.

"I don't care. Nothing too serious, though. Maybe a comedy?"

Harold flipped through the channels until he settled on a sitcom, hoping a little irreverent humor might lighten his mood.

It didn't take long for the wheezing to start. Harold turned his head toward the recliner next to him, where Sharon was leaning back and snoring loudly.

He felt a surge of disgust rise in his throat as he gazed at her. The woman he had fallen in love with years ago was gone. In her place was a lazy, unkempt, and overweight sloth that had given up on herself and her appearance. She looked nothing like the beautiful, vibrant, and fit woman he had vowed to cherish and protect.

Even as he thought this, his eyes wandered down to his

own gut, which protruded from underneath his shirt. He had always been a little on the big side—he was big-boned—but sadly, his spare tire had grown a little over the years. He blamed this on Sharon as well. Because of her, he had given up a lot of things that he used to do. The gym that he used to work out at regularly was now a distant memory. The net on the basketball hoop in their driveway had disintegrated a long time ago, not from use but the elements, and he had not been motivated to fix it. Hell, he didn't even go fishing anymore, something he used to do religiously. In short, Harold had lost his passion for life. His dreams had faded into oblivion, and it was her fault.

Sharon jolted awake in the recliner as Harold's hand shook her gently. "Why don't you go up to bed, Hon?" he said.

She looked around with a groggy and bewildered expression, completely disoriented. She felt a dryness in her throat and a pressure in her eyes. Sharon swallowed hard and rubbed her eyes, trying to shake off the sleepiness.

"Are you okay, Hon?" Harold asked, more out of common courtesy than genuine concern.

Her reply was coarse and scratchy. "I don't feel too good. I think I'm coming down with something."

Of course, you are dear.

"Mind if I go up to bed?"

Of course, not dear. "No, not at all," he said.

"Don't stay up too late, okay?"

I'll stay up as long as I fucking want to! "I won't."

Harold cringed as he watched Sharon drag herself up the stairs, making loud and pitiful noises with every step. When she was gone, he slumped on the couch for a while, flicking through the channels without paying attention to anything. Bored and restless, he finally turned off the TV and got up from the couch.

***

A soft hum issued from the computer as Harold sat in the corner of the den, surfing through a few porn sites. After a few minutes, he came across one with a banner ad for Sweet Temptations, the same dating site that had bombarded him all day. He freaked out for a second, but then his curiosity got the best of him. As his palms grew sweaty, he craned his head closer to get a closer look at the model exposing herself on the screen, and was suddenly sucked into the monitor.

A second later, Harold was standing at the front of a line before a long counter. On the wall behind the counter was a sign that read SWEET TEMPTATIONS in bright red letters. Below the sign was a long menu board separated into two categories: SENSUAL and KINKY, with several sexual and deviant fantasies listed under each one.

A tall blond with large breasts in a skimpy uniform stood behind the counter like a cashier at a fast-food restaurant.

She winked at Harold, "What'll it be, Handsome?" she said with a slight Southern drawl.

Harold stood there, speechless.

"You don't have to be shy, sweetie," the girl urged. "We're here to take care of you."

Harold stuttered, "But...but I've never done anything like this before."

"Ah, I see. This is your first time. We have just the thing for you."

The cashier pressed a button on the counter and a moment later, a tall brunette, dressed in the same skimpy uniform, walked out of a door off to the side and approached Harold.

"This is Cindy. She can make all of your dreams come true, Harold, but only if you let her."

It shocked Harold when he heard his name. "How do you know my name?"

The cashier winked at him again before Cindy grabbed his arm and led him toward a hallway off to the side.

"Come on, Harold," Cindy said, as she put her arm around his waist and let her hand slide down to grab his ass. "Let's have a little fun."

Chapter 16

Michael felt a cold sweat on his forehead as he watched Cindy pull Harold out of the lobby. She stopped at the door and turned her head to face Michael, showing him a horrific smile that exposed her jagged teeth and dripping tongue. Her flesh was rotting and peeling, her eyes were burning with malice, and her hair was a writhing mass of worms.

The cashier wore the same demonic face and addressed Michael, "Don't worry, pretty boy! We've got something special in store for you."

Without warning, the floor cracked and split, revealing a dark abyss below. Terror surged through Michael as he saw dozens of pale and bony hands reaching out for him from the depths. Before he could scream, they clutched his leg and yanked him down into the blackness with an irresistible force.

A moment later, Michael's eyes snapped open, and he gasped in horror. He was strapped to a huge wooden wheel, his limbs stretched out and secured by metal chains. The room was a nightmare of shadows and sinister instruments, like a medieval dungeon of horrors. In front of him, a cruel Mistress smirked wickedly, holding a whip with razor-sharp spikes. "You know you don't belong here, right?" she hissed.

"Please, I don't know what's going on here!" Michael whimpered. "Can't you just let me go?"

The woman chuckled, "Now, what would be the fun in that? Besides, Belial would be upset if he found out I didn't whip some sense into you."

With a violent tug, she shredded Michael's shirt to pieces with her sharp claws, exposing his bare chest. She dragged her nails along his skin, leaving behind bloody gashes that stung with pain.

The demonic dominatrix walked behind Michael. Her pointed heels struck the stone floor sharply, while the ominous whistling of the whip as it slashed through the air bit at Michael's ears in a warning. Then, the barbs on the whip pierced the air with an eerie whisper before they gouged deep into his flesh. Michael let out a bloodcurdling scream as his veins pulsed with excruciating pain, his mind consumed with terror.

***

With gentle grace, Cindy guided Harold into a spacious and opulent room, complete with a grand fireplace that dominated one of its walls. As they walked, the room was filled with soft, sensual music emanating from hidden speakers ensconced in the ceiling. And there, at its center, was an extravagant king-size bed, positioned directly in front of a roaring fire.

"Why don't you lay down, while I slip into something a little more comfortable?" Cindy said.

As Harold made his way onto the bed, his movements

betraying an awkward uncertainty, Cindy departed for the adjoining bathroom. Her absence was fleeting, however, as she soon returned, donning a white lace teddy that stressed every curve of her body. In that moment, Harold's throat went dry, his nerves intensifying with each beat of his heart.

Cindy frowned, "Are you still nervous?"

Harold replied, "A little."

"Well, then, how about a drink to relax?"

Harold nodded. "A drink sounds good."

Cindy scooted off the bed, baring her ass for Harold. She grabbed the bottle of champagne from the end table and opened it, giggling as the cork flew up and hit the ceiling. She filled two glasses and returned to the bed, handing one to Harold.

"Here's to fun and happiness, Harold," she said as she clinked her glass with his in a toast.

Harold downed his drink quickly, while Cindy took a sip of hers and put her glass on the table. She took Harold's empty glass and put it beside hers.

"Are you feeling better?" she asked.

Harold replied softly, "A little."

Cindy looked deeply into his eyes, "What are you afraid of, Harold?"

Harold shrugged, "I don't know?"

"Well, if you were to die tonight, what would be your biggest regret?"

Harold looked at the goddess beside him. "Not being with you."

Cindy smiled and climbed on top of Harold, straddling him, "I was hoping you'd say that."

Harold closed his eyes as she bent down to kiss him, only to open them a second later with the disappointing realization he had fallen asleep in front of his computer.

"Well, that fucking sucks!"

He sighed as he shut the computer down and left the room, his heart empty and bleak.

Once upstairs, he took off his clothes and laid them gently on the floor beside the bed before slowly crawling under the covers, careful not to disrupt his wife. She wasn't snoring now, but if he disturbed her, even slightly, that could change in an instant. Then he wouldn't get any sleep.

Within a few minutes, Harold approached the brink of sleep. As he prepared for the night's journey, one thought kept reverberating through his mind: *Oh, how I wish my life was different!*

Chapter 17

The gentle flicker of sunlight on Harold's eyelids coaxed him out of his slumber. He rubbed his eyes for a moment, letting the rest of his senses adjust to the new day. The pungent odor of stale beer invaded his nostrils, and it startled him as he took his hands away from his eyes and realized that he was lying smack-dab in the middle of a flesh sandwich. A blond girl was lying naked on his right side, while a brunette lay naked on his left. Each one was lying on her side so that her ass touched Harold's legs.

A big smile spread across his face as he looked at the ceiling. "God, if this is a dream, please don't wake me up!"

He glanced over at the nightstand next to the bed. Empty beer bottles and drug paraphernalia adorned the top of it and immediately brought a sharp pain to his groin as he realized he had to piss badly! "Don't move, girls," he said. "I'll be right back."

Harold crawled his way to the foot of the bed and stumbled his way to the bathroom. After relieving his bladder, he stood in front of the mirror, running his fingers through his hair. "Best moment of my life!" he said with an uncontrollable smile.

Puffing his chest out and sucking his gut in, he tried his best to make himself look sexy as he strutted back into the room. He climbed back onto the bed enthusiastically. "Okay girls, time for some more fun!"

Neither of the women stirred.

But he was determined to wake them. His fingers caressed the contours of the brunette's supple waist behind him while he kissed the tender flesh of the blonde's nape in front of him. Still no movement.

"I guess I wore them out!" Harold said proudly.

Harold turned up the intensity a little, reached around, and massaged the blonde's breasts while he backed himself up to the brunette and began to grind on her.

"Come on, girls, I know I'm new to all this partying stuff, but I'm loosening up. I promise I'm a fast learner."

Still nothing.

Harold, becoming increasingly agitated, pulled the blond closer to him so he could reach her more easily. Her head drifted sideways and a cry of horror flew out of his mouth as the girl's dead eyes stared back at him. A trail of blood had dried from her nostril to the corner of her mouth. The other nostril still had a trace of a powdery white substance showing. A small glint of light attracted Harold's eyes to the razor blade on the nightstand next to an undisturbed line of cocaine. For a brief second, a thought entered his brain, *That wasn't there before!*

Terror ran rampant through Harold's mind as he leaped out of the bed. As he did, the body of the other girl fell sideways. The same dead eyes that belonged to the blond now lived in the brunette's head. However, instead of a trail of blood on her face, a multitude of bruises covered the girl's neck.

Harold heard a muffled cry from the side of the room and walked over to see Cindy lying there in a pool of blood with a knife sticking out of her stomach. He rushed over and cradled her in his arms.

"My god, Cindy! What happened?" he cried.

Cindy's voice shattered as she clung to the last shreds of consciousness. "Don't you remember?" she gasped.

Confusion reared its ugly head once again in Harold's brain, "Not really."

A volley of blood spewed from Cindy's mouth as a wave of gurgled coughs tore through her. When the fit had passed, she looked up at him with hatred burning through her eyes. "It was you, Harold. You did this!"

Harold gaped at her in horror. Then a torrent of images flooded his mind, but they didn't belong to him. It was more like he was trapped in a nightmare, with himself as the doomed hero.

He saw the four of them partying together, a heated mixture of drugs, sex, and rock-and-roll. He watched in his mind as he enjoyed the full pleasure of the three girls in his bed, their bodies all covered with sweat. He saw the blond bowing her head, almost in reverence, as she sniffed at the white powder eagerly. Then, as her body started convulsing violently, and the blood ran, the brunette became hysterical and started screaming.

Harold reached for her slender neck, hoping to silence her screams, but his fingers had tightened like a vise around her delicate skin, while his eyes had glazed over with terror, and in a matter of heartbeats, the two girls lay motionless and pale before him.

A shrill scream pierced the air as Cindy brandished a large blade, ready to defend herself. Harold, driven by fear and desperation, lunged at her, hoping to wrestle the weapon away. But in his haste, he pushed it deep into her flesh, feeling her warm blood spill over his hands.

Then, a surge of terror and vertigo overwhelmed him, and he plummeted between the two corpses on the bed and blacked out.

After the initial shock of what he imagined might have happened subsided, Harold returned to his present reality, holding Cindy in his arms as her last gasp of air left her lungs.

For a long time, he sat there in disbelief, mumbling to himself, "My God, what have I done?"

Finally, he laid Cindy's body on the floor and crawled over to his clothes, which were scattered across the floor. *Get ahold of yourself, Harold!* He thought as he crammed his clothes on. *This is all just a dream! It has to be. Any second now, you'll wake up.*

Harold squeezed his eyelids shut, hoping to escape the horror, and let out a pitiful sob when he peeled them open again to find it still looming over him.

He snatched up the phone and fumbled with trembling hands to dial 911.

A woman's sharp and distinct voice answered almost immediately, "911, what is your emergency?"

The voice on the other end of the line pierced Harold's mind like a knife. He babbled and raved, spewing out words that made no sense, his voice cracking and trembling. "They're dead, all of them! I don't know what happened! I just woke up, and they were there! I can't believe—"

"Calm down, Sir," the woman said. "Take a deep breath and tell me what happened. Let's start with your name."

Harold fought to regain his composure, but his mind was racing like a wild beast ready to break free from its cage, clawing and biting at his sanity. He had to force his words to come out slower, "My name is Harold."

"All right, Harold. Why don't you start from the beginning and tell me what's going on?"

"I don't know what's going on! The last thing I remember was falling asleep last night next to my wife. Then I woke up and there were three dead women in my room with me!"

He felt the terror rising back in his throat as he finished that last sentence.

"Can you tell me where you are, Harold?" the woman asked. "We can have an officer there shortly."

"I swear I didn't do anything!"

"I'm not saying you did, but if there are dead bodies present, we need to get an officer there immediately. Can you please tell me your address?"

Harold gulped and said softly, "It's 1917 Leer Street."

The phone went silent for a second before the dispatcher spoke up again. "I'm sorry Harold, but I'm not showing a 1917 Leer Street anywhere on our map. Are you sure you have the correct address?"

"I'm positive! I've lived here for ten years. I think I know my own address."

The woman's voice remained calm and professional, "But, Harold, we don't have a listing for a Leer Street anywhere in Los Angeles."

"What do you mean you don't—"

He stopped mid-sentence as those last few words registered in his brain. "What did you just say?"

The woman's voice held a hint of confusion. "I said that I'm not showing a Leer Street anywhere in Los Angeles."

The first time he heard it had stopped him short. The second time almost floored him. Without realizing it, he flopped back onto the bed, almost landing on top of one of the girls. He flinched as he felt her cold flesh brush against him. Right now, that didn't concern him as much as the fact that he actually lived in Indiana, not California!

Chapter 18

The dispatcher tried desperately to keep him on the line. "Stay with me, Harold! We'll have someone there shortly. Just stay on the line and everything will be all right."

The image of Sharon flashed before his eyes, and he let go of the phone in a frenzy. He dashed out of the bedroom, his feet pounding on the floor. The hallway reverberated with his desperate shouts of her name.

Harold stopped dead in his tracks when he came to the end of the hall. Normally, he would've run down a flight of stairs to the first floor. Instead, he found himself at the entrance to a cavernous room. A gleaming black marble floor mirrored the sun streaming through the skylights above. Various pieces of exquisite art contrasted the dazzling white walls, while sumptuous leather furniture adorned the entire room.

The sharp smell of chlorine lingered in the air, and Harold spotted a pair of massive glass doors to his right that opened up to a patio. A sparkling swimming pool tempted him from beyond. Harold glanced out the window for a moment and saw the remnants of a wild party that had gone on, with empty beer cans and clothes scattered around the area carelessly.

What caught Harold's attention the most, though, was the photograph hanging on the wall next to the patio doors. He recognized the picture immediately, or at least part of it. It was his wedding night. There was no mistaking it. The tuxedo was the same, his hair was the same, and even his goofy smile was the same. The woman standing next to him was not. In the place where Sharon's image should have been, there was someone else. Instantly Harold recognized her as the dead blond woman in the bed.

He became nauseous as he bordered on the verge of a nervous breakdown. Apparently, he had killed his wife, only it wasn't really his wife...and he wasn't really here...and none of this was really happening...

Harold tried everything to escape the nightmare. He jerked his head from side to side, squeezed his eyes shut, and pressed his fingers against the bridge of his nose. He even chanted the phrase, "this is all just a dream", over and over. But when he opened his eyes again and saw that nothing had changed, he realized with terror that this was his new reality.

Loud banging nearby broke Harold's mania, and he felt a surge of panic. He cautiously walked back into the hallway toward the patio doors. As he got closer, he saw a young woman with dark, wet hair clinging to her face, wearing a white bikini. She was pounding on the doors desperately. "Please, let me in!" she cried. "She's after me!"

Harold tried to peer around the girl through the glass, but couldn't see anyone else.

She continued frantically. "Please, Harold, you have to let me in!"

It stunned Harold for a second when she mentioned his

name before he opened the door.

The girl rushed in and put her arms around him, squeezing him tight. "Thank you! I knew you'd save me."

"How do I know you?" Harold asked.

"Don't you remember? It's me, Samantha? From work?"

Harold drew a blank.

Samantha continued, "You invited me to your party last night?"

Harold shook his head.

Suddenly, the tip of a knife blade shot out of Samantha's eye from behind. The other eye held a look of shock as she slumped to the floor.

Harold screamed in terror as he faced the abomination that had once been his beloved Sharon. She leered at him with a grotesque smile, revealing jagged teeth that dripped with black bile. Her skin was a deathly blue, covered in thick veins that writhed like worms under her surface. She looked like a corpse that had been submerged and mutilated in the darkest abyss, and now she had emerged to claim his soul. Water bubbled from her mouth as she spoke. "You couldn't just be satisfied with what we had, could you, Harold? Instead, you had to throw it all away for some bimbo. I hope you're happy now?"

Harold slowly backed away from her, pleading desperately, "This is all a big mistake, Sharon. You have to believe me. I don't know what's going on here!"

"I've put up with enough of your shit, Harold! Time for you to join your little bimbo slut here in Hell."

Sharon reached down and yanked the knife out of Samantha's skull. With a crazed yell, she lunged for Harold.

Harold recoiled, barely dodging Sharon's savage attack before he whirled around and dashed for the living room. The noise of her waterlogged feet smacking the tile floor, mingled with a howl of rage, haunted him like a banshee down the hall.

When he finally reached the door, he looked back over his shoulder one last time and saw that Sharon was gone. It took every ounce of courage left in him to walk back down toward the hall.

Harold cautiously peered around the corner, expecting to have a knife plunged into his chest at any second, but ghoulish Sharon was nowhere to be found, as was Samantha's dead body.

He ambled back toward the front door, hoping to find some answers, but not even sure what the questions were anymore.

He gripped the handle and braced himself for what unspeakable things might lurk on the other side. Sweat dripped down his forehead as he battled with his fear. Finally, he sucked in a deep breath and counted to three. Then he pulled hard, and the door flew open.

The scene outside was lush and ripe, not like the six inches of snow that had buried his sidewalk at his actual home the night before. The bright noon sun was a solitary figure in the blue sky above. Birds chirped happily. Squirrels chattered at each other like gossiping women. Harold thought that this place would be paradise if not for the horror that rested inside.

Harold's heart pounded as a squad car skidded to a halt in the driveway. His panic rose to a fever pitch when the officer stepped out of the car and strode toward him. He was the tallest and darkest man Harold had ever laid eyes on. The stubby mustache under his nose and the mirrored sunglasses he wore gave him an intimidating aura. He wondered what those eyes were hiding behind those glasses and shivered.

As the man loomed over the steps, Harold's stomach

dropped. He felt like a tiny insect under his shadow, about to be smashed. The officer stood silently in front of Harold for a minute, surveying the situation. His mouth opened, and a deep, raspy voice came out, "I got a call that there was a problem here."

In contrast, Harold's voice squeaked as he talked, "I don't know what happened! I didn't do anything! You gotta believe me!"

"Why don't you show me what the situation is, boy, and I'll decide what to believe?"

Harold's throat constricted as he let the officer inside. The man's arm grazed Harold's hand as he passed, and Harold pulled back from the searing heat that radiated from the officer's body. It felt like touching a burning iron.

The officer fixed his eyes on Harold with a cold and menacing stare, "Are you just going to stand there, or are you going to show me the bodies?"

Harold nervously made his way past the officer and led him down the hallway. That the swimming pool and surrounding area were free of debris both relieved and unnerved him. Finally, he arrived at the bedroom door and took a deep breath before pushing the door open. He backed quickly into the hall again. The officer sighed as he walked into the bedroom.

A minute later the officer called out, "Harold, is it? Can you come in here, please?"

Harold stepped into the doorway and looked up at the towering man, who was blocking his view of the room beyond.

The man looked at Harold sternly, "You're telling me, you have no idea what happened here?"

"Yyess, sir," Harold gulped.

Harold could almost hear the cop's eyeballs rolling around

in their sockets. "So, let me get this straight. You're saying someone else came in here while you were sleeping, killed these women, put two of them next to you in bed, handcuffed the third one to the end of the bed frame, wrote that filth all over their bodies, and you didn't see or hear a god-damn thing?"

Harold peered around the officer in confusion. The girls were still there, as cold and dead as before. He thought he saw a slight change in their faces, though. It could've been his imagination playing tricks on him, but he could swear that the corners of their mouths were turned up just a little in a morbid grin.

That wasn't what shocked him, though. It was the fact that there was now writing all over the girls' bodies. The words 'bitch', 'slut', and 'whore' were repeated over and over in black ink.

Cindy was lying on the floor at the foot of the bed with her left arm handcuffed to the frame, with the same words written on her body. She showed no sign of the knife wound, but her mouth was drawn up in the same sly smile, like she had taken a devilish secret with her to the grave.

"Those weren't there before!" Harold blurted out defensively.

The cop raised an eyebrow at Harold, "What do you mean, those weren't there before? You already said that you woke up this morning with these dead girls in your room."

"No, not that! The writing wasn't there before! And the other girl was lying on the floor in the corner, not handcuffed to the bed!"

A frown spread across the officer's face, "I'm afraid I'm going to need you to come with me."

The words struck Harold with the sting of a right hook to his temple. "But I didn't do this! You've got to believe me!"

"The only thing I got to do, Boy, is my job!"

The officer yanked Harold by the shoulder and spun him around. The sharp metal of the handcuffs bit into Harold's skin as he locked them on with a cruel smirk and hauled him out of the room.

"This is all just a big mistake!" Harold cried. "I could never kill anyone!"

The officer ignored his pleas as he led Harold out of the house and shoved him into the back of his squad car. "Never is an awfully long time, Harold," he said.

A pack of boys, no older than ten, skidded their bikes to a stop and gawked as Harold was thrown into the back of the cop car. They all sported black shirts and shredded jeans. Their blood-red hair stuck to their foreheads from the scorching heat, as if they had been riding in the sun all day. They were the spitting image of each other, including their eyes. Their eyes were jet-black and voracious, revealing their true nature

The first boy laughed, "Haha! Look at that loser! I bet he's a real creeper!"

The second boy said, "Yeah, I bet he did something real bad, like murder or something."

Then the third boy chimed in, "Creeper perv. I hope he gets what he deserves."

The boys started chanting loudly, "Creeper perv! Creeper perv! Creeper perv!"

The officer smiled at the boys, then started whistling as he walked around the front of the car. It was an upbeat tune, triumphant in its melody.

Chapter 19

The images flew through Michael's brain in rapid succession —the blond girl's body shaking violently while a stream of blood pours down her chin; Harold squeezing the life out of the brunette as he's caught in a web of panic; then accidentally plunging the knife into Cindy's stomach. Michael watched the entire scene unfold before him in the elusive and surreal way dreams do. In a flash, the girl's dead eyes were staring up at him. Then, in unison, the three girls winked at him. He wanted to scream, run, close his eyes, turn off the projector in his mind, but even in the most basic of nightmares, these are all impossible.

An instant later, Michael stood outside under the bright California sun as the police officer emerged from his vehicle, a black swirling mass of muscle and evil. Initially, he was the silent observer in this horror story. But, as the officer approached the front door to the house, he turned and looked right at Michael. His eyes were fire, and he looked at Michael as if he was looking into his soul.

A feeling of panic overwhelmed Michael as he beheld the

monster before him. The officer responded with a wide toothy grin that revealed razor-sharp teeth lining his mouth and told Michael that this was no man at all.

Suddenly, Michael was in the corner of the bedroom again while Harold rambled desperately on the phone, trying to explain the horror of the dead women in the room with him. After Harold left the room, running frantically in search of a sanctuary that didn't exist, Michael watched spellbound as the 'dead' women suddenly sprang to life and oddly moved their fingers over each other's bodies. They giggled like pubescent schoolgirls during an all-night slumber party, while their gestures and undulations magically became black ink on their skin.

A moment later, Michael was back outside and watched as the officer yanked Harold from the house in handcuffs and shoved him into the back of the police car. Then the officer walked straight up to Michael and removed his sunglasses. His eyes were pitch black for a second before they turned to fire red.

The officer grinned the same razor-sharp, toothy grin. He turned toward the three boys, who returned his smile with the same razor teeth lining their mouths. "Hey boys, looks like we have a peeping Tom on our hands. What do we do to peeping Toms?"

The three boys responded in unison, "We spill their guts and eat them for dinner!"

"That's right, boys. We spill their guts and eat them for dinner."

He turned back toward Michael. "What do you think, piss-ant? Should we spill your guts and eat you for dinner?"

The officer chuckled and walked back to his car, leaving Michael trembling.

***

Sirens blared as a caravan of police and emergency vehicles arrived at the scene. A detective got out of the lead car, followed by a dozen other officers and CSI emerging from the others.

The Detective approached the officer and peeked inside the rear window of the squad car at Harold. He raised an eyebrow and shook his head, "God, what a loser!"

The officer chuckled, "Yeah, tell me about it! He'll suit my purpose, though."

The detective looked doubtful. "You sure? Well, it's your plan. What's the scene inside look like?"

"You'll love it. Nice and juicy."

The Detective laughed for a second before he paused and walked toward Michael, peeling the skin from his face as he went. Blood oozed down the man's fleshless face as he approached Michael.

"Were you aware you had a visitor?" the detective said over his shoulder.

The officer replied, "Yeah. I'm aware."

Michael tried to move but was paralyzed. The Detective reached a bloody hand up and ran a sharp nail along the edge of Michael's chin, slicing his flesh open.

"I could take care of him if you'd like?" the detective said with a wide grin.

"No. Leave him for now. I need to see what's going on with him. I don't think he's acting alone."

The Detective shrugged, "Suit yourself," and walked toward the house.

***

After settling himself in, the officer reached for his radio and called the station. Instead of dispatch answering, screams of torture blared through the speakers. "No need for back-up," he said matter-of-factly.

A female voice interrupted the screams, "Roger that, Boss Man."

"Situation's under control. Going to lunch now."

"Sounds good," the voice hissed. "Preparations are under way."

Harold's eyes widened in fear as he watched the exchange unfold. His face paled, and his lips trembled as he struggled against the handcuffs that bound his wrists. He twisted and turned frantically, his muscles straining against the metal restraints. His breath came in short, ragged gasps, and his heart pounded in his chest.

The officer turned the radio off and reached up to adjust the rear-view mirror so that he could see Harold's face. A broad smile erupted on the black man's face, his white teeth gleaming back at his prisoner in the mirror. His voice changed a little as he spoke, his excitement visible in his words, "You okay back there, Harold?"

"No, I'm not fucking okay!" Harold cried. "What do you mean, the situation is under control? It doesn't seem under control to me! And what was that screaming in the background?"

"You need to calm down, Harold. That's the only way you're going to get through this."

Everything was spiraling out of control, "I'm telling you for the hundredth time, Officer, I didn't do this! How can you expect me to stay calm?"

The officer remained cool, almost polite even. "Don't worry, Harold. We'll fix you up real good," then, as an afterthought, "and please, call me Reverend. Everybody else does."

The pit in Harold's stomach was now a bottomless abyss. *I certainly don't like the sound of that!* He thought.

They had been driving for what felt like an eternity, the officer's tune ringing in Harold's ears like a mocking laugh. He looked around and realized they had escaped the city's watchful eye and were now in the middle of nowhere. The officer's whistling turned into a manic frenzy as he swerved the car onto a dusty path. The sky darkened in an instant, and a fierce wind shrieked as lightning cracked and thunder boomed.

Harold's breath caught in his throat when he witnessed a spider crawl out of Reverend's ear and vanish into his hair. Reverend began to claw at his scalp where the creature had hidden, and his hair came alive with a horde of wriggling legs and eyes. He slid his glasses down his nose and fixed his gaze on Harold in the mirror. His eyes were gone, replaced by blazing infernos that burned into Harold's soul.

"Don't worry, Son," Reverend said in a sinister tone. "Everything will be over soon."

His gaze then turned back toward the road and he asked a peculiar question in a peculiar voice, "Are you a God-fearing man, Harold?"

Harold was speechless for a moment. "I guess so," he finally answered softly.

"See! That's the problem with people today—no conviction! Either you are or you aren't!"

As if to amplify the officer's statement, a loud crash of thunder ripped through the sky, followed by streaks of lightning amidst a torrent of rain.

The car came to a halt. Harold peered out his window and felt a chill as he saw a massive, dilapidated barn looming ominously before them. The red paint had flaked off, exposing the rotting wood underneath. The roof was riddled with holes. One of the sliding doors had fallen off its hinges and leaned against the barn like a tombstone. Reverend got out of the car and dragged the other door open with a loud screech. The darkness inside was thick and suffocating, ready to engulf Harold in its deadly embrace.

Harold's heart stopped as Reverend returned to the car and bared his teeth in a demonic grin—the split tongue of a serpent darting from his mouth. The terror that Harold had felt earlier was nothing compared to the nightmare that seized him now.

As soon as they entered, Reverend leaped out of the car, flicked a switch and a dim light cast a faint glow over the front of the vehicle. The barn was filled with the low hum of a generator, and a lone chair stood in the center of the floor, only a few steps away from them. It seemed to smile at Harold with its high back and raised arms, like an executioner's chair waiting for its next victim on death row.

Reverend dragged Harold out of the car with a savage force and hurled him onto the chair. Harold made a desperate attempt to escape, but was instantly pinned down by Reverend's iron grip. His arm came around, and the back of his hand met Harold's cheek in a resounding blow, ripping his flesh open as the ring on his finger cut him deep.

Little wisps of smoke danced from the fibers as Reverend wrapped a rope around Harold's hands and feet. Another strand around Harold's chest secured him to the chair, while a third around his neck completely immobilized him.

Harold tried yet again to plead with the lunatic cop, his

mouth the only part of his body able to move. "Please, you've got to believe me. I didn't do anything! I swear, I don't know what's happening. I never saw those girls before in my life! Please, just let me go!"

Reverend glared at Harold, his temper rising, "How stupid do you think I am? How can you sit there and tell me you never saw those girls before when I saw a picture of you and your wife hanging on the wall?"

He took a deep breath for a second to calm himself. "Would you like to know why everyone calls me Reverend?"

The only sound coming from Harold in response to his question was a series of weak cries.

Reverend stood silent for a moment, deep in his pride. "I have a way of making people see the folly of their ways. I bring illumination to them. And you, my friend, need to see the light badly."

For a moment, Reverend stepped back and looked at Harold as if he was admiring his handy work. Then he sauntered back to him, shaking his head back and forth. He took his glasses off and Harold saw his eyes completely for the first time. A cold, hard, icy blue, which hardly seemed natural in that body.

Reverend bent down and stared into Harold's eyes with a piercing intensity. His words came out in a spray of saliva, as if he were spitting poison from his fangs. "Why don't you tell me why you did it, Boy? Maybe we can save ourselves a lot of trouble."

Harold's words were drowned by the tears gushing down his face, filling his mouth with a choking sound as he spoke. "I'm telling you the truth! I didn't do anything! This is all just a big mistake!"

A flurry of punches rained down hard on Harold. Reverend glared at him for a moment. "Look! We can do this the easy way, or we can do this the hard way! It's up to you!"

"I'm telling you; I don't know what happened! Why won't you believe me? Do you want me to confess? Is that it? Do you want me to say I did it? Okay, I did it! Are you happy? Will you please let me go now?"

"I don't believe you!"

Reverend reached into his pocket and pulled out a knife. With an evil smile, he flipped the blade open. "Since you won't talk to me, how about if I make sure you can't talk to anyone else, ever again?"

With his free hand, he reached into Harold's mouth and pulled out his tongue. The gleam in his eye matched the gleam coming off the switchblade as it swung down and sliced Harold's tongue off.

Harold's throat tightened and he let out a muffled scream as the agony ripped through his veins. His limbs trembled uncontrollably and his vision blurred as he felt the first signs of shock taking over his system.

Chapter 20

Harold blinked as the shadows gradually faded, revealing his surroundings. He was on the witness stand, the defendant in a trial. The courtroom was overflowing with hateful eyes, shouting and cursing at him. Sharon was sitting at the prosecutor's table, no longer the water-logged demon that had tried to kill him earlier. Now she was dressed like a woman scorned, with cold eyes and a determined jaw. Her attire was composed of a red, low-cut blouse that seemed to scream to Harold, 'Look at what you threw away!'

Beside her was a tall man in a dark suit with his hair slicked back. He sat there with a smug look on his face.

Seated at the defense table was Benny, dressed in a pinstriped suit and white tie. His face bore the expression of a man who knew the battle was lost, but was trying his best to give Harold a semblance of hope.

A loud smack sounded that startled Harold, and he turned to see the judge, a middle-aged man with long blond hair, pounding a gavel furiously on his desk. A hint of familiarity squeaked into Harold's brain, but quickly escaped his grasp.

"Order! Order!" the Judge demanded. "Everyone quiet now or I'll have this courtroom cleared!"

The room grew quiet, and the Judge turned to Harold, "You've heard the accusations against you, Harold. What do you have to say for yourself?"

Harold sat there confused, not sure what to say.

The Judge continued, "This is your chance to set the record straight, Harold. If you refuse to cooperate, I'll be forced to hold you in contempt."

"But...but I don't know what's going on here?" Harold said, his voice creaking weakly.

"Are you saying you don't understand the charges brought against you?"

Harold shrugged as his head slunk low, "I guess so."

The Judge looked down at a pile of documents on the podium, canvasing through the records for a few moments, and then looked up, "Well, it is a pretty long list, so I can see where you might get confused. First, we have murder, which is pretty self-explanatory. Then we have involuntary manslaughter, which is a little more complicated. After that, we have a wrongful death charge, followed by rape, the influence of a minor, drug possession, under the influence of an illegal substance, public intoxication, lying to an officer, obstruction of justice, adultery, and finally, just being an all-around dick."

Harold sat there, speechless.

"I'll take your silence as testimony that you do, in fact, understand these charges," the Judge declared.

The Judge turned to the prosecuting attorney sitting next to Sharon. "Does the prosecution have anything else they'd like to add?"

The slick-haired man stood and said with a silver tongue, "No, Your Honor. The Prosecution rests. The evidence is clear that the defendant is guilty, and we feel confident the jury will come to the correct verdict."

The Judge addressed the defense team. "Does the Defense wish to say anything else at this time?"

Benny rose from the table and winked at Harold. "Yes, your honor," Benny said as he approached the jury, which consisted entirely of females.

Benny spread his arms out wide, "Ladies of the Jury, we've listened to a lot of terrible accusations thrown at my client today. Some of them are worse than others, but all of them are bad. Now, before you come to any kind of conclusion about Harold's guilt or innocence, I want you to take a good long look at him right now. Does he look like a person who could commit such terrible atrocities? I mean, come on, he's a weak and pathetic excuse for a human being, sure, but last time I checked, being pathetic isn't against the law. It's just sad. The evidence against him is circumstantial at best, and for that reason, you must find him not guilty."

Benny smiled at the jury before he sat back down at the table. He folded his hands together before him and winked at Harold as if to say, 'we got this'.

The Judge addressed Harold once more. "Do you have any last words for the court, Harold?"

Harold looked at Sharon with tears running down his cheek, "Please, help me. We can fix this. I didn't do any of those things they said. I don't know what's going on here. It's all just a big misunderstanding."

Sharon regarded him coldly. "Why should I help you, Harold? In our twenty years of marriage, you've never appreciated me for anything I've done, you inconsiderate fuck! You deserve whatever comes to you."

The Judge cringed, "Ouch!"

The crowd started murmuring, while Harold sat there in

silence for a moment before answering, "You're right. I'm sorry."

Sharon replied, "Too little, too late."

After the judge dismissed Harold from the witness stand, he addressed the Jury, "You've heard the testimony today. Now it's time for you to reach a verdict. Please, take your time deliberating. Remember, a man's soul is on the line."

The Jury got up and proceeded out of the courtroom, each woman glaring at Harold as they left. They returned almost immediately and took their seats.

Benny whispered to Harold, "A quick verdict is never a good thing. But, keep your fingers crossed anyway."

"Has the jury reached a verdict?" the Judge asked.

The head juror stood up. She strongly resembled the dead blond woman in the bed with him when this nightmare started. Then he realized that all of them were replicas of the three dead women, and he felt himself slipping further into darkness.

"We have, Your Honor," the woman said.

"Good. And what is your decision?"

The women all turned toward Harold and said in unison, "Guilty on all counts!"

The courtroom went wild with the announcement, and the Judge pounded his gavel for silence once more.

The room grew quiet, and he turned to Harold. "Harold, you have been found guilty of all charges against you. The sentence for these crimes is immediate death!"

The Judge turned to the bailiff and guard standing to the right of the bench, both of whom were colossal men eager to execute the Judge's orders. "Please escort Harold to the execution chamber, where he will face a swift death by beheading."

The two men approached Harold and yanked him roughly

from the witness stand.

Harold pleaded desperately as they dragged him toward a door in the room's corner, "But I'm innocent. Why won't anybody believe me?"

The Judge replied, "It doesn't matter whether or not you're innocent, Harold. The jury has spoken. Their word is the law. What kind of judge would I be if I went against their verdict? And so, now you die."

The two men pulled Harold through the door into the room beyond. Harold's eyes grew wide when he saw the glint of the guillotine blade winking at him. He tried to pull away feebly, but the men held him tight.

He was crying hysterically as they forced him to his knees and placed his head in the restraint below the large blade. He tried to plead again, but he was too weak.

A minute later, he watched as the audience from the courtroom filed in and took a seat in a row of chairs near the edge of the platform that the death apparatus rested on. They hooted and hollered like they were gathering at a show for their amusement instead of someone's execution.

The Judge approached Harold and kneeled before him with a smug expression on his face, "Any last words before it's all over?"

The only words Harold could utter were, "I'm sorry."

The Judge patted Harold's cheek lightly, "I'm afraid in this case, that's just not good enough. Goodbye, Harold."

He gestured to the Bailiff, who had stationed himself next to the lever mounted on the wall that unleashed the enormous blade looming above. The Bailiff smirked and yanked the lever, while the crowd erupted with frenzy.

Harold heard the clink of the chain as it released the blade from its perch and braced himself. A split-second later, he felt the sharp steel bite into his flesh and everything went black.

***

Blood oozed from Michael's mouth as he watched the man in his dreams torture the helpless soul that was Harold. He fell to his knees, weakened from the blows that resounded across the victim's face. When he felt the blade bite into his neck, he reeled from the terror.

Michael watched feebly as the man, bound like a captured animal, teetered on the brink of death. Then, when Harold had lost consciousness, the sinister being who called himself 'Reverend' turned and walked directly toward Michael, grabbed him roughly by the hair, and pulled his face toward him.

"Do you know who I am, boy?"

Michael attempted to mutter something weakly and then realized that his own tongue was missing. Reverend laughed wickedly before releasing Michael. He then bent down and looked Michael in the eyes. "It doesn't matter, though. My plan will succeed in the end."

Chapter 21

A cheerful, victorious whistle tore through Harold's ears and snapped him awake. He grasped at a faint hope, for a brief second, that his world had restored to normal. But when he opened his eyes, that hope was immediately shattered.

"Ah, Mr. Wagner, you came back to us, after all. You had me worried for a second there."

Harold tried to blink the blood out of his eyes, to no avail. He opened his mouth to speak, but only a muffled sound trickled from his throat. Then he remembered that his tongue was gone!

"Awe, what's the matter? Cat got your tongue?" Reverend laughed. He leaned in close, his breath smelling like death.

Harold's eyes grew wide as he watched the face before him change. The nose thinned, the eyes grew softer; the lips became fuller, and the hair grew longer. After a few seconds, he was staring at Sharon's face, smirking back at him.

Then it changed again. The wicked smile remained, but was now surrounded by the hard lips of a man. His jaw was firm and chiseled. Long, gold hair flowed down to his shoulders, and his eyes became sapphire blue.

The man made a little bow of showmanship. His voice was sharp and hissed as he talked, "Belial the Fallen, at your service."

What do you want from me? Harold thought.

"Why, my dear Harold, I want your soul, of course!"

No! This can't be happening! It isn't real!

"But I'm afraid it is real, Harold. It's all very real." He brought his hand up to touch the side of Harold's face. Harold winced as the heat from Belial's hand made his flesh smolder and the wounds ooze once more.

Belial extended his hand, palm open, so that Harold could see his dismembered tongue lying there, looking more like a giant slug instead of a human organ. Belial snapped his fingers and Harold's tongue was restored. "You see, I need your help to put my plan into motion. But, don't worry. The price you pay will be worth it when you become one of my chosen four to lead this world into a new age. I guarantee, Harold, you will be magnificent!"

Harold started sobbing again. "Why me?"

"I chose you for a very special purpose, Harold. Your whole life has been one disappointment after another. But I'm going to transform you into something magnificent that will make Heaven and Earth fall to their knees! Once I've secured the others, together you will become an unstoppable force."

Harold just whimpered and cried again.

Belial bent down and whispered warningly in Harold's ear, "You will be mine!"

***

Harold bolted upright in bed. His shirt was soaked with sweat, bringing a chill to his already trembling body. He took a deep breath, trying desperately to keep his pounding heart from jumping out of his chest.

After a minute, the whirlwind subsided. Everything seemed back to normal. Sharon lay next to him, fast asleep. The alarm clock glowed 3:33 from its normal perch atop the nightstand. He even heard snow plows off in the distance, working diligently throughout the night to uncover the city from the recent snowstorm.

Harold inched his way over the side of the bed and made his way to the bathroom. He squinted hard as his eyes struggled to adjust to the bright light.

God, what a nightmare!

He turned on the water, just a little. The cold splash felt good on his face as it brought his senses back to reality.

As he looked at his reflection in the mirror, the terror of what he thought had been a nightmare flew back into him harder than ever. It wasn't so much the scratches on his face that troubled him. He could have easily scratched himself, tossing and turning in a fitful dream. Even the fact that his tongue hurt wasn't out of the ordinary. Everyone has bitten their tongue once or twice in their sleep. But the bruises on his neck and face were different!

For a long time, Harold sat on the toilet trying to figure out what had happened. Then he realized that the 'what' wasn't as important as the 'why'.

He remembered the feeling of desperation he had the day before and the stress that had surrounded the entire house last evening. He recalled the thoughts that filled his head as he lay down to sleep, and a wave of guilt engulfed him. He had betrayed everything that he had once held dear.

Harold sat there in quiet contemplation for a long time,

trying to make sense of everything until he realized that he'd been given something that most people never get—a second chance. He vowed at that moment to make the most of it.

As he walked back into the bedroom, Sharon sat up in bed, the grogginess in her voice apparent, "Are you okay, Hon?"

He leaned over as he sat on the edge of the bed and kissed her lightly on the forehead, "Everything's fine, dear."

Her astonishment was clear at Harold's gesture. It grew even more when he kissed her softly on the tip of her nose before moving down to capture her lips. Instantly, the passion flared between them, and they felt a scorching desire rekindle that had vanished a long time ago. They surrendered to each other in a passionate embrace, leaving nothing unsaid and nothing undone.

Both of them sweaty and exhausted, Sharon nestled beside Harold on the bed, feeling his warm skin and his rapid heartbeat. She breathed in his scent, a mix of sweat and cologne, and smiled softly. He wrapped his arm around her and kissed her hair, whispering words of love in her ear.

"I missed this," Sharon said, as she nestled a little closer to him.

"Yeah, me too," Harold replied.

"I'm sorry I've been such a bitch to be around lately. I've just had a lot on my mind."

"It's okay, Sweetie. I'm sorry if it seems like I've been taking you for granted. I don't mean to."

Sharon sat up and kissed him again. When she pulled away, her eyes were misty.

"What's wrong, Dear?" Harold asked with a hint of concern in his voice.

Sharon was silent for a moment. "I didn't know how you'd take it, so I didn't tell you."

"Tell me what?"

She looked him in the eyes for a long second. "I'm pregnant."

Harold was stunned for a moment, unsure how to react. A million questions swarmed through his brain. *Another child? How are we going to manage? Can we afford it?*

He flashed back to the nightmare that had haunted him; the one that had almost broken him. And he realized that he had the strength to overcome anything life threw at him. He smiled and kissed her again, holding her tight, feeling her warmth and love radiating through him.

Chapter 22

Sharon was busy making breakfast while Casey sat in the corner of the room, absorbed in her coloring book. She didn't hear Harold sneak up behind her and wrap his arms around her waist, pulling her close. He nuzzled her hair and kissed the back of her neck softly, making her giggle.

"Morning, Beautiful," Harold said.

Sharon replied, "Well, good morning!"

Harold looked over her shoulder at the pancakes and bacon cooking on the stove and took a deep whiff. "That smells delicious!"

"It'll be ready in a minute. Grab a cup of coffee and I'll bring it to you."

Jared bounded into the dining room and joined Harold at the table as he sipped at his coffee.

"Where's David?"

Jared replied scornfully, "Who cares?"

"Hey!" Harold snapped. "What did we talk about last night?"

Jared lowered his head. "I'm sorry. He should be down in

a couple minutes."

David joined them a minute later, just as Sharon sat plates of food onto the table. Casey walked right behind her, delicately trying to balance a small plate of toast in her hands. She beamed with pride as she put the plate on the table without spilling it. Then she sat down in her chair and eyed the food hungrily.

As everyone dug into their plates, Harold looked at Sharon, who was glowing, and smiled. He nodded his head to her slightly with a question in his eyes. She nodded back. "Hey boys, how would you feel if our family were to get a little bigger here pretty soon?"

David looked up excitedly, his mouth full of food. "Are we finally getting a dog? What kind? Is it a puppy, or is it full grown?"

Harold chuckled. "No, we're not getting a dog. And before you ask, it's not a cat either."

Jared looked back and forth between his mom and dad for a second, before a light-bulb went off in his head. "No way! Mom, are you pregnant?"

Sharon nodded her head. "Yes, kids, you're going to have another brother or sister."

David shook his head and laughed. "Boy, you guys really are gluttons for punishment."

Harold looked at Sharon and smiled. "Yeah, I guess we are."

***

As he drove to work, Harold felt a surge of emotions that he had forgotten a long time ago. He turned the radio up to the max, belting out the lyrics to every song like he was a rock star on a stage. He didn't care about the stares and glares from other drivers, he just laughed them off. He had his family back, and he was determined that nothing would ruin his mood again.

Minutes later, as Harold put his briefcase on his desk next to his computer, Jeremy's head popped up from the other side.

"Hey, Harold, how's it hanging?" Jeremy asked.

Harold beamed as he replied, "Actually, it's hanging pretty good right now, Jeremy."

Jeremy smiled. "You old dog! You got some last night, didn't you?"

Harold blushed.

"Good to see you still got it in you," Jeremy teased.

"Hey, I never lost it, pal."

Jeremy laughed. "Have you reconsidered my offer for the barbecue this weekend?"

"Yeah, we'll be there. Sharon has to watch what she drinks, though."

For a second Jeremy was confused, then his eyes lit up. "Are you saying what I think you are?"

"Yep. Sharon's pregnant."

Jeremy came around the partition and gave Harold a hug. "That's fantastic! Congratulations, man!"

"Thanks."

Johnathon, a tall and obnoxious guy in his thirties, who walked around with his chest puffed out like he was better than everyone else, approached Harold's cubicle. "Hey, what's going on?" he asked haughtily.

Jeremy replied, "Harold's going to be a father!"

"I thought he already was?" Jonathon said.

"No, you idiot! He's going to have another baby. His wife's pregnant."

Johnathon sneered at Harold. "No offense, Harold, but I

didn't think you could still get it up? I guess you won't be checking out the new help, then?"

Harold asked, "What new help?"

Johnathon directed Harold's eyes to the corner of the room, where a woman was sitting with her back to them. She turned and Harold's stomach dropped when he saw Cindy looking back at him.

"Her name is Candace," Jonathon continued. "Just moved here. Man, I'd sure like to taste that!"

Harold slumped into his chair with a soft gasp, his eyes wary and frightened as if he had just seen a ghost. "Sorry, I need to get going here. I got a big client lined up and I still have a lot of prep to do. I'll talk to you guys later."

"Sure, no problem, pal," Jonathon said. "I was just about to go introduce myself, anyway."

Jeremy turned toward his own desk. "Yeah, I got some work to do too. Glad to hear about your news, Harold."

Harold held his breath for a minute before he dared to raise himself from his seat and spy over the rim of the cubicle toward the front. A surge of relief flooded through him as he realized it wasn't Cindy, but a doppelganger. He dropped back into his chair and let out a shaky breath.

After pulling up the appointment calendar on his computer, Harold came across the name, Brandi Tahapenes. He looked at the name curiously for a minute before he dialed the number to confirm the appointment.

After a couple of rings, a bubbly female voice answered, "Sweet Temptations. How can I help you?"

A lump immediately formed in Harold's throat.

After a moment of silence, the woman spoke up again. "Harold is that you? Are you calling to make up? Well, it's too late for that! Look me up when you're burning in Hell and we'll talk!"

The line went dead.

Harold ripped his headphone off and tried to run from his desk, but tripped on his chair and fell to the floor.

Minutes later, Harold felt a hand on his shoulder and opened his eyes to find that he'd fallen asleep at his desk. Jeremy stood next to him with a concerned look on his face.

"Man, she really must've worn you out!" Jeremy said. "It's a good thing the boss didn't find you asleep like that."

Harold sat up in his chair and looked at the clock in shock. It was almost five o'clock. He had lost an hour!

"Yeah. I don't know what happened?" Harold replied. "All of a sudden, I was just out."

"Are you okay?"

"I'm fine. Just beat."

"I feel ya. Say hello to Sharon for me."

Harold simply nodded as Jeremy walked back around to his own desk.

*****

Harold bounded up the steps as he hurried into the house. The boys were fighting as usual, but he barely heard them. The only thing on his mind was Sharon. His search ended when he found her in the laundry room, with Casey on the floor next to her helping 'fold' clothes.

Harold snuck up behind her and squeezed her tight, kissing her gently on the back of the neck, and sending chills through her body.

"Good afternoon, Gorgeous," he said.

Sharon turned around and smiled, "Good afternoon yourself, Handsome."

The boys stopped their fighting and looked at them in surprise. "What's gotten into you two?"

Harold and Sharon just smiled, leaving the boys rolling their eyes and making gagging gestures as they left the room. Casey, however, wanted in on the affection and held her arms up toward them.

Everything is just like it used to be; just like it should be, Harold thought. He swore to himself that it would stay that way.

After dinner, Harold rushed to the living room and turned on the TV just as a basketball game was about to start. Right before tip-off, Sharon strolled into the room with the boys in tow. "We need to go to the mall for a little shopping. Do you want to come?"

Guilt covered Harold's face. "There's a big game on tonight I've been looking forward to all week."

Sharon looked at Harold's pouting face and laughed. "Don't worry Hon. It's no big deal."

Casey saw everyone else getting their coats on and ran to the closet to get hers. Sharon looked at her and smiled, "Okay, little girl, you can come too."

"Don't stay out too late," Harold said. "It's a school night."

Sharon replied, "We should be home in a couple hours. I hope your team scores lots of touchdowns."

Harold chuckled as they headed out the door into the chilly winter evening.

***

The loud knock on the front door brought Harold sharply awake just in time to see the final score: Notre Dame 62 UConn 60. A little smile spread across his face, even though he was disappointed that he'd fallen asleep.

He glanced at his watch and saw that it was almost ten o'clock. *Sharon and the kids should've been home a long time ago. It's past Casey's bedtime, and the boys have school in the morning.*

Another loud knock hit the door just as Harold was about to turn the handle. *Who in the world could be knocking at this hour?*

His heart sank when he saw the two police officers standing on the porch under the dim light.

One officer spoke up right away, "Harold Wagner?"

"Yes, that's me. Why? What's going on?"

"I'm sorry to have to tell you this, Sir, but there's been a terrible accident."

Harold's knees buckled, and he had to grab the door-frame to keep from collapsing. His words stumbled out of his mouth, "What kind of accident? What happened? Are Sharon and the kids all right?"

The officer looked at Harold for a second. His expression told him everything, even before the words came out of his mouth. "A truck ran a stoplight just as your wife was leaving the shopping mall. There was nothing the emergency crew could do to save them. I'm terribly sorry."

The words pierced Harold's heart as he plummeted to the ground. He lay frozen on the porch for a timeless moment, paralyzed and shattered. Then he felt a wave of agony engulf him and he cried out in despair, his tears gushing down his face in a torrent.

Both officers reached down and helped Harold to his feet. Slowly they worked their way into the house, where Harold fell back onto the couch like something had ripped out his spine.

The second officer spoke up, "Is there anyone we can call for you, a friend or relative maybe?"

The words struggled to reach Harold's mind, his emotions clogging his mental pathways. He turned his pale face toward the officer with a blank expression and somehow forced out in broken words and sentences that their families were scattered across different states. There was no one else to call.

After trying to console Harold, the second officer spoke up again before they left. "When you feel up to it, we'll need you to come down and identify the bodies. But only when you're up to it."

Harold answered with a vague grunt, and the two officers walked out of the house, leaving Harold completely alone.

Wave after wave crashed down on Harold. His heart burned and his soul ached like he hadn't thought possible. Just when his ocean of sorrows had calmed just a little, so that he might bring his head back above water and not drown in the swirling abyss, another wave slammed down hard, sending him reeling. It was only when they were gone that he realized how much they had truly meant to him.

Finally, a long time later, the tears ran dry and his mind went numb from the terrible blow it had endured. Somehow, Harold found the strength to stand and willed himself up the stairs toward his bedroom. The only thought in his head was that maybe, if he laid down for a little while, he would wake up and it would all be just a bad dream like before. *Yes! This is all just part of the same nightmare! I'm going to wake up any second now.*

Harold didn't seem to notice that the light was already on in the bedroom as he tried to flip the switch. Then he stumbled toward the edge of the bed and was startled to see a small piece of paper lying on his pillow. Curiously, he picked it up and unfolded it. It was the flyer from Sweet Temptations with a message written on it: 'I told you so!', signed with a smiley face sporting a pair of horns.

Harold sat down on the edge of the bed absently rubbing the side of his face and the front of his neck, feeling the emotional and physical scars there. His tongue rolled lazily around in his mouth, and he felt the soreness that was still there. Then he realized there was only one thing left for him to do.

He dropped to his knees beside the bed and reached under it for the locked box hidden there. He fumbled with his keys for a second before he found the right one. Slowly, he withdrew the revolver from inside. His hands were eerily steady as he loaded the bullets into the gun. He spun the chamber before putting the barrel of the gun into his mouth.

Belial's voice echoed through the room, "Careful what you wish for, Harold! You just might get it."

Quietly, Harold said a last goodbye to his wife and children. Then he pulled the trigger.

***

Michael's eyes were flooded with tears as he watched the shattered man lying on the bed from the corner of the bedroom. He felt the hollow emptiness in Harold's soul. He shared in his agony, and he related to his torment. How many times had he wounded the people who loved him? Spurned those who tried to help him? And when he had lost them irrevocably, how the remorse had torn him apart like a savage animal? He realized too late that regret was a curse that would haunt him forever.

***

The loud bang of the gunshot echoed through Michael's nightmare and jerked him back to reality. He lay motionless on the couch for a long time, quivering violently. His hair was soaked with cold sweat that trickled down his forehead and neck. His mouth was dry as a bone and his tongue felt like sandpaper. A freezing coldness and a gnawing emptiness invaded his bones that made him shudder.

After a while, he calmed down a little and stumbled on weak legs to the bathroom, where he found the familiar bottle of aspirin and the small bottle of whiskey hidden in the medicine cabinet—his best friends the last few weeks.

As he stood in front of the mirror, searching for answers, Belial's words resounded in his brain: "Do you know who I am, boy?"

Without warning, the mirror's surface began to undulate like a disturbed pond. Michael felt another surge of fear as he witnessed a chaotic montage of hellish creatures and heavenly beings clashing in a fierce war. He recognized Belial among the horde of demons, his eyes glowing with malice. The vision culminated with the piercing wail of a newborn child.

Suddenly, Michael gasped in agony. He pulled his shirt up and twisted so he could see his back in the mirror. Deep gashes ran across his skin, still oozing blood. He heard the crack of the whip reverberate once again in his mind just before it tore at his flesh.

Michael slunk to the floor crying hysterically. He was so weak and tired. But something told him that Belial was just getting warmed up.

Chapter 23

Jacob, a short and round ten-year old boy with a plain face, sat at the table with a party hat on his head, gazing at the birthday cake in front of him with wide eyes.

Next to him sat his mom, Betty, a portly woman, while his aunt, Janice, equally big, sat on the other side of him.

Standing throughout the room, each one waiting anxiously, were several friends and relatives, all large and hefty.

While Janice lit the candles on the cake, Betty brought up a bag from the floor at her feet. "I got you something, Little Piggie."

Jacob's eyes lit up when she pulled a stack of masks from the bag: little pig noses with a rubber band stapled to each side. She placed one around Jacob's head and then passed them around to everyone.

"Time to make a wish, Little Piggie."

Jacob closed his eyes for a second and then blew out the candles. Everyone in the room responded with a series of loud snorts.

Betty leaned over and kissed him lightly on his cheek. "Happy birthday, Jacob! Dig in! This is all for you, my sweet Little Piggie."

Jacob buried his face in the cake and started gobbling up eagerly. As he gorged himself, the pig snorts grew louder throughout the room.

***

The buzz of the alarm clock woke Jacob up. He was still short and round, but now ten years older. After slamming the top to turn the alarm off, he laid in bed, curled on his side with soft tears streaming from his eyes.

After a minute, he reached for his phone and saw that he had a voice-mail. He hesitated for a minute before he finally listened to the message. 'Happy birthday, Sweetie. Hope you have a great day! Love you!'

Jacob sighed as he hung up his phone and climbed out of bed.

***

As he had done all of his wretched life, ever since he was a defenseless boy, the man who had been branded with the name of Wheezy, or sometimes Squeezy Wheezy, or Little Wheezy, because of his short and rotund frame and his debilitating asthma, faced a harsh world as soon as he crossed the threshold of his front door.

He took a deep breath to prepare himself for whatever assault would come his way as he started walking toward his job at the corner grocery store. Not that the walk was difficult —the trek itself was only a few blocks—or even that he lived in a bad part of town. The problem was Ben Whitaker's house. It was situated directly in the middle of his route and was the primary source of his anguish. If it wasn't asshole Ben himself causing trouble, it was his two sons, who weren't any better.

Jacob took a quick hit from his inhaler as he walked down the steps from his tiny apartment building. A silent prayer echoed through his brain every step he took that he'd get past the house without incident.

And he almost made it. Almost.

He was about ten yards from the edge of the property, which was a goal line of sorts to him, when the two brothers came out of the house, both wearing dirty white t-shirts smeared with oil and grease.

Caleb was the first one to see Jacob. Tall and skinny, with unkempt hair and the beginning of a peach-fuzz mustache, he was a year older than his brother, Trent. He was also the meanest of the two.

As soon as he saw Jacob, he grinned and reached down to pick up a large rock. Trent followed his example, like a little brother usually does, and picked up a rock of his own.

"Hey, Squeezy Wheezy!" Caleb yelled. "Where you going?"

Jacob kept his head forward and continued walking. A second later, He cried out when a rock hit him squarely in his back.

"I asked you a question, you fat fuck!" Caleb continued.

Another rock whizzed past his ear, coming dangerously close to his head. He picked up his pace, hoping to get far enough away that they'd give up. Each step was tinged with a spear of pain right between his shoulder blades.

He was startled by the sound of pounding footsteps closing in on him from behind. A sudden jolt of pain shot through his skull as something slammed into the back of his head. He whirled around, dizzy and disoriented, and glimpsed Trent's smug face and clenched fist. He was laughing maniacally as he delivered the blow. Caleb followed his brother's assault with an uppercut to Jacob's jaw.

The force of the punch knocked Jacob off his feet and hurled him to the pavement. He crashed down with a thud, feeling his bones rattle and his flesh scrape against the rough concrete. His skull cracked hard against the cement, causing lights to dance around his eyes before he passed out. He only vaguely heard the brothers teasing him as his hearing became muffled.

"That'll teach you to ignore us, you fat fuck!" Caleb said. Trent started to say something else until he realized Jacob wasn't moving. "Holy shit!" he said. "I think we really hurt him."

When blood started seeping into the sidewalk surrounding Jacob's head, they backed up. "Let's get the hell out of here," Caleb said. "Dad's gonna beat our asses if he sees this."

They fled the scene, leaving Jacob helpless on the ground. He was bleeding out, his body limp and lifeless. His vision blurred and his mind went blank as he fell into nothingness.

***

Jacob slowly regained consciousness and found himself lying on a stiff hospital mattress. The pungent odor of antiseptic assaulted his nostrils, making him wince. He swallowed hard, his throat burning from the bile that had risen during his ordeal. A sharp pain shot through his left hand from the needle embedded on the top that was feeding the drip from an IV into his veins. He struggled to clear the haze that clouded his mind as he forced himself to sit up, but a wave of excruciating pain crashed over his skull. He screamed, falling back onto the pillow.

"I wouldn't do that if I were you," a female voice said from across the room.

He turned his head slowly toward the source and saw a petite red-headed woman in a nurse's gown walking toward him wearing a name tag that read 'Terri'.

"Where am I?" Jacob asked weakly.

"You're at Valley Medical Center," Terri replied.

Jacob vaguely remembered the attack. It had happened so fast. What he did remember clear as day, though, was the awful sound that echoed through his ears as his skull hit the sidewalk—the sharp, wet thwack that signaled impending trauma. Then, a moment later, nothing.

He reached his right arm up and dabbed the back of his head, feeling the bandages there wrapped around his head.

"You suffered an acute subdural hematoma because of the skull fracture that happened when your head hit the sidewalk," Terri told him.

Jacob said, "Well, that doesn't sound like fun."

"Do you remember what happened?"

He had a clear picture of what had most likely transpired, knowing the cruelness that resided inside the Whitakers. He didn't see the details, because he had been facing the other way. The dilemma was, though, if he spoke up and the brothers faced the consequences, they would make him pay with double the brutality. So, he kept his mouth shut and lay there motionless.

Terrie frowned, sure that he was holding onto something he shouldn't. "It's okay. Sometimes things are foggy for a while with an injury like yours."

"How long have I been here?" Jacob asked.

"A little over two weeks."

Jacob's eyes grew large. "Two weeks?"

Terri nodded, "Because of the pressure on your brain, the doctor put you in a medically induced coma until the swelling receded."

Jacob was stunned, "What about my job...and my apartment...and my—"

Terri put her hand on Jacob's shoulder to calm him down. "Take it easy, Jacob. Everything's fine. We've already contacted your employer. Look over in the corner."

An impressive collection of flowers graced the surface of a small table. Some of them had inspiring balloons tied to them, cheering him on to get well soon, while others had heartfelt cards tucked inside, expressing their love and care. He smiled gently, feeling the moistness of tears on his face.

Terri wiped his eyes and cheeks. "Don't get all choked up here, Jacob. You're gonna make me cry, too."

"It just feels good to know people care," he said softly. "I haven't felt like that for a long time."

"Well, from the looks of it, a lot of people care about you, Jacob. I know I do."

Jacob was shocked at the last part of her statement. "But you don't even know me."

"Yes, I do," she said with a smile as she walked to the door. "Get some rest now. I'll come back in a couple of hours to check on you."

She plunged the room into darkness as she exited, leaving Jacob alone with his thoughts. He tried to recall the face of his enigmatic nurse, but his mind was foggy from his trauma, and he couldn't summon any clear images. He drifted off to sleep again, hoping to see her in his dreams.

Chapter 24

The next morning, Jacob woke to find Terri sitting in the chair next to him.

"How are you feeling?" she asked him as she stuck a thermometer into his mouth before wrapping the blood-pressure cuff around his arm.

"Still tired, but better," he mumbled.

After a minute, she removed the thermometer and frowned. "Your temperature's a little high, but your blood pressure's fine. Do you still have a headache or any dizziness?"

Jacob started to reply, but his vision quickly became blurry, not from losing his focus, but because blood was running down his forehead and into his eyes, blocking him from seeing. Panic gripped him with a sudden force, and he gasped for air as his breaths grew shallow and ragged. "What's happening?" he cried.

Terri was trying to staunch the flow of blood when Dr. Bellhorn came in. "So, how are we feeling today?" he asked without looking up as he scanned over Jacob's chart.

"Oh, my," he said when he finally saw the state Jacob was in. "That's not good. Grab the extra bed linens from the cabinet," he directed Terri.

"We need to get him to the OR. STAT!" Terri said emphatically.

"No time!" he said. "We'll have to fix this here."

While Terri did her best to slow the flow of blood, the doctor rifled through the workstation behind the bed. When he returned, Jacob's condition had worsened so much that he resembled a bubbling macabre fountain befitting a haunted house attraction on Halloween. His hospital gown had turned a deep shade of red. The bed and floor were both soaked in blood. There were even splatters of blood on the ceiling from the spray.

The doctor brought the attached tray up from the side of the bed and swung it around so that it created a shelf under Jacob's chin. Then he moved around behind him, holding a pair of forceps in one hand and a scalpel in the other. "Now, let's see if we can figure out what the problem is here, Jacob?"

"Try to hold him steady," he said to Terri, who promptly pressed on Jacob's shoulders to hold him down.

Jacob tried to move under her weight but found her strength too great for him in his weakened state.

"Now, you're going to feel a little sting," Dr. Bellhorn said as he slid the blade of the scalpel down the middle of his scalp. The doctor whistled a happy little tune as he cut deep, causing another geyser of blood to flow.

The 'sting' was a fire burning itself into Jacob's brain as he felt the blade penetrate his flesh. He tried to cry out, but the doctor pressed a little harder at one point, and Jacob suddenly found that the only part of his body he could move was his eyes. He was completely paralyzed!

Jacob felt the tug of his flesh being pulled open as the

doctor pulled his scalp apart with the forceps, all while still whistling happily. Then he watched in horror as pieces of his skull were plopped onto the tray in front of him. Within seconds, a pile of bone and brains lay before him.

Dr. Bellhorn then exclaimed, "Ah! I think I've found the culprit!" He reached the forceps into Jacob's brain, twisting it around like he was fishing for a wedding ring dropped into the garbage disposal. Finally, he grabbed hold of his target and pulled.

A silent scream was all Jacob could muster as the pain seared through him.

One last quick yank and the doctor held his prize in front of Jacob's face—a large, worm-like creature nearly two feet long, that had a circular mouth filled with needles. The thing wriggled angrily under the doctor's grasp. "There, that should take of it. You should be all good to go."

He bent close to Jacob. "Don't worry. We'll be seeing each other again real soon."

He watched as the doctor walked out of the room, with Terri following behind. She stopped at the door and turned to him. "Try to get some rest, sweetie. You look like hell!"

She flipped off the light and everything went black.

***

Jacob shot up in his bed, only to regret it instantly. The terror had provoked his reaction, and he paid the price in spades. The nightmare had been so lifelike; so horrifying. He wrestled to relax himself, but then he felt it, the stabbing pain in his brain again, like the knife slashing through his skull.

Her voice cut through the darkness enshrouding him, bringing a sliver of peace to his tortured soul, "It's okay, Jacob. It was just a dream," then he felt a soothing hand on his and turned to see Terri sitting next to him. He offered her a weak smile, still shuddering from his dream. Even as the nightmare faded from his consciousness, he knew that there would always be a tiny splinter of it concealed in the gloom, waiting to taunt him again. Somehow, he knew this ghost would never set him free.

She brought a glass of water up to his lips. "Take a little sip. It'll help."

He tried to take the glass from her, but his hands were trembling. She guided the rim of the glass to his lips and he gulped down a couple of sips before his head fell back to his pillow in exhaustion.

"How long have you been there?" he asked.

"Long enough," she replied.

"Can you stay with me for a while? I don't want to be alone right now."

"Of course, I'll stay. Even if you don't remember, you helped me out a long time ago. Now, it's my turn to help you. I'll be here as long as you need me."

Her fingers clutched Jacob's hand, giving him a much-needed anchor, and as he peered into her eyes, he saw a tiny spark igniting there. The warmth emanating from her calmed his mind and after a few minutes, he drifted into a restless sleep, his thoughts escaping to find memories of the angel sitting next to him.

Chapter 25

As the first rays of sunlight peeked through the curtains, Jacob opened his eyes and saw Terri slumped in the chair beside his bed, her head resting on her folded arms. He took a moment to admire the way her hair cascaded over her shoulders and the gentle curve of her lips. She looked like an angel to him, the most beautiful person he had ever seen. She shifted slightly and blinked, meeting his eyes with a sleepy smile.

"Did you sleep here the whole night?" Jacob asked.

She rubbed her eyes awake and stretched the kinks out of her back and arms. "I told you I would. How are you feeling?"

"Better. Thank you."

"I'm glad. Hopefully, we can get you out of here soon so you can get your life back to normal."

"Yeah, normal wasn't all that great for me."

Terri frowned, "I'm sorry. That's not what I meant. If it's any consolation, they found the two brothers that attacked you. There was a witness nearby who reported the incident.

The cops picked them up later that same day."

A little smile spread across Jacob's lips, "Serves them right."

Terri looked down at her watch. "Shit! I have to start my rounds. I'll come back later and check in on you again."

As she was rushing for the door, Jacob said, "I remember."

Terri stopped. "You remember what?"

"We were at Northwood Middle School and you were being bullied by a couple of other girls. One of them—can't remember her name—pushed you down, knocking your glasses off. I was walking by and helped you up."

"You were the only one who ever helped me at that school. Nobody else gave a damn."

"Yeah, I know the feeling."

"We didn't see each other much after that since our classes were always different, so I never got the chance to say thank you."

"I think what you've done here more than makes up for that."

She smiled at him before turning toward the door. Then she stopped and looked back over her shoulder. "Her name was Nancy Rose, and she's still a stuck-up bitch. She got what she deserved, though. Had a kid when she was sixteen, ended up on welfare, and now lives with a loser of a boyfriend who treats her the same way she treated everyone else. I guess what goes around, comes around."

***

As the clock on the wall ticked mercilessly, Jacob felt his heart sink lower and lower. He had been counting the minutes, the seconds, for her to appear, but she was nowhere to be seen. He knew he was being unfair—she had other lives to save, other duties to fulfill—but he couldn't shake off the pang of doubt. Her company, her voice, her touch, was better than any of the drugs they had pumped into his veins.

A smile of relief covered his face when she finally peeked her head inside the door. "I have some bad news," she said, quickly turning his smile to a frown. "I won't be able to see you anymore today. I just had another bad case given to me and it's going to take the rest of my shift."

"Well, that sucks!" Jacob replied.

"But I talked to the head nurse," Terri told him, "And she's agreed to cut my case load down for a little while so that I can devote more time helping you with your recovery."

Jacob grew concerned. "How long is my recovery going to take?"

"It's hard to say. The concussion from your fall alone is probably going to take a couple more weeks. Then we have to deal with the effects of the coma. Your muscles are going to be atrophied, so you'll need to go through physical therapy to get your strength back up. My goal is by the end of the month you're able to walk out of here."

The prospect of spending another month in the hospital filled Jacob with dread, but he had no say in the matter. The only silver lining was that he'd get to see Terri more often. She was the only ray of sunshine in his gloomy existence, the only reason he had to live. "As long as you're here to help, I guess it'll be okay."

"I have to warn you, though, that it's not going to be easy. I'm going to be hard on you, push you to get stronger. Just remember that it's for your own good."

"Whatever you need to do. I trust you."

"You say that now..."

***

Terri appeared the next morning, radiant and energetic, just like she had sworn, and then every morning following that. And while Jacob was overjoyed to see her, he soon discovered that her visits would not be all sunshine and butterflies. She tested him harder than he'd ever been tested before, demanding he put every drop of his blood and sweat into his recovery.

It all paid off.

Nearly three weeks to the day after Terri peeked her head in and told him her plan, she walked beside him as he exited the building and headed toward a waiting taxi.

"I'm proud of you, Jacob," she said when they stopped at the rear door of the vehicle.

"I couldn't have done it without you," he replied.

Then she caught him off guard with a move he never expected. She tilted her head and brushed her lips against his. A fleeting but gentle kiss, but one that spoke volumes. Then she handed a little slip of paper to him.

"Call me," she said before she turned around and walked back into the building.

Jacob was smiling as he climbed into the backseat of the cab. He opened the note and saw a phone number written on it. It was signed with a T and a little heart beside it.

The driver, an older man with long, blond hair, glanced at Jacob in the rear-view mirror. "She seems like a keeper, Jacob," the man said.

It startled Jacob. Something about the man seemed familiar, and not pleasantly. A brief image from his nightmare rocketed into his brain, only to disappear before he could catch it. "How do you know my name?" he asked.

"I overheard the nurse mention it. I think she likes you."

"You think so?"

"She wouldn't have given you her number if she didn't want you. If you play your cards right, you might get a little piece of that action."

Jacob didn't respond. He knew the guy was suggesting something purely physical, but Jacob felt it was more profound than that. He had felt a strong connection—deep feelings, if you will—and hoped she reciprocated them. Of course, the gnawing doubt was there that he was simply the product of the Florence Nightingale syndrome. But he didn't want to dwell on that. He'd let things unfold as they would.

After a few minutes, they stopped in front of his apartment building. As Jacob looked at the property, he realized just how depressing it was. He hadn't cared much before. Now, it was different. He didn't want Terri to see him living in a dump. For the first time, he felt embarrassed to live there.

The driver said, "Yeah, it's a real shit-hole, isn't it? But on the bright side, the asshole kids who lived down the block won't be causing anyone else anymore problems. Heard they got offed by a couple of gang members in jail while they were running their mouths. Serves them right, if you ask me. The world could do with a few less scabs on its ass."

It shocked Jacob when he heard that the Whitaker boys were dead. Sure, they were dicks, but he never wanted anyone to die.

He started to get out of the cab and then stopped as he searched through his pockets, but came up empty. "I don't have any cash to pay you for the ride," he said.

"Don't worry about it. That little woman of yours already covered it. Just make sure you do the right thing and call her. She's gonna make big things happen, I can promise you that."

It took Jacob three days to get up enough nerve to call Terri, and when he finally did, he was all flustered and tongue-tied. He wasn't exactly a Casanova with women, after all. But when everything was all said and done, she agreed to go out with him.

That moment made all the torture he had suffered worth it. It started his life on a positive trajectory that he never could've imagined. Love has a way of doing that. It spilled over into everything. He excelled at his job and was promoted to department supervisor in charge of Produce. Later, he moved into a better apartment in a nicer part of town, bought himself a nice used car, and asked Terri to marry him.

When she said yes, he felt like his life was finally the way it should be. He went from a life of shit to a life filled with promise and hope. But hope is a fickle bed partner to lay your head with.

Chapter 26

Michael jolted awake, feeling a searing pain in his skull. The remnants of the nightmare were fading fast from his mind, but there was one thing that tormented him; one thing that was imprinted on his brain like a tattoo: those ice-blue eyes. He had seen them gazing at him from the doctor's expression, and before that, the man on the ledge, and then in Reverend.

This latest episode felt like it was heading down the same trajectory as the first two, and Michael didn't know if he had the will to withstand another onslaught. Also, Mary wasn't there to help him this time.

He needed something badly to dull the pain, and he needed it right now. The bottle of vodka was still on the kitchen counter, tempting him like a siren song. Fear had stopped him from moving it then, and fear stopped him from touching it again now.

Michael sighed. In Philly, there was only one place he could go to make sure he got what he needed: Kensington and Somerset. He didn't like the idea of venturing out so late at night into the worst part of town, but he felt desperation inching itself closer like an ex-girlfriend dressed in a slutty outfit looking for a quick score. Luckily, his crappy apartment on Frankford was only a few blocks away.

Michael threw on a gray hoodie to warm him against the cool night air and ventured out in search of a friend. What he needed was anything to help dull the ache in his mind.

After a couple of blocks, he cut through a yard onto Seltzer Street and then made his way toward Jasper. As he rounded the corner, he heard the sounds of gunfire interrupting the night a few blocks away. The noise itself wasn't uncommon in this neighborhood, given its history of drugs and violence, but in his present state, it unnerved him.

He made it halfway down the block when he heard a male voice call out, "I wouldn't go that way if I were you."

Michael looked around and could barely make out a dark figure sitting on the stoop of a worn-down building. The streetlight on the corner cast a deep shadow across the structure, making the figure appear tall and lanky as he stood up.

"I'm warning you, Michael," the guy continued. "There's nothing but disaster waiting for you if you continue down the same path you're going."

Now, Michael had no choice but to stop. "How in the hell do you know my name?" he asked as he walked toward the mystery man.

Instead of answering, the man simply turned and walked up the steps into the building, disappearing a second later inside.

"Don't worry about him," another voice said behind him. "He's always sticking his nose into other people's business."

Michael spun around to face a towering black man in a brown fur coat. His fingers glittered with gold rings, while a gold chain draped around his neck. The man's eyes were dark and cold under the harsh glare of the street-lamp. "Can I help you with something?" he asked.

The man replied, "Michael, is it? Actually, I think I'm the one who can help you,"

Another series of gunshots rang through the night not far away. "The old man was right about one thing, though. I wouldn't go that way. They're lighting the night on fire right now."

Michael looked dejected. He needed his fix, but now he'd have to find another source, and soon.

The man put his arm around Michael. "Hey, don't look so down. If you need help, then I'm your guy. They call me the Rubber Band Man, and I got whatever you need."

The Rubber Band Man backed away and threw his coat wide. Multiple pockets lined each side, loaded with bags of every kind of drug possible.

Michael's eyes lit up for a second, and then he hung his head down low in embarrassment. He wasn't strong enough to fight the demons raging inside him on his own, and this was the only way he knew how. *What would Mary think right now if she saw me? Hell, she'd probably leave me. And she'd be right, too.*

The man lifted Michael's chin, and for the briefest of moments, the eyes were ice blue before changing back. Michael brushed it off as a reflection from the light, but it unnerved him.

"Hey, don't worry what other people think," the Man said. "I say fuck 'em. Unless they've walked in your shoes, they have no idea what shit you're dealing with. And I can tell, my man, that you're dealing with some heavy shit. Am I right?"

Michael nodded slowly.

"I like you, Michael. You seem to be a good guy who's just

going through some stuff. I'm gonna help you out."

He reached into one of his coat pockets and pulled out a little bag filled with white powder tinged with red. "This is from my personal stash. It's some of my finest work, if I do say so myself. I call it Maelstrom. I guarantee a couple hits of this and you won't feel a thing."

Michael started to reach for his wallet, but the man stopped him. "Hey, this one's on me. You just have to promise me one thing."

"What's that?" Michael asked.

"That you'll stop fighting and embrace the abyss as it calls to you."

Michael didn't understand what the man was saying and brushed it off as he reached for the bag. He simply nodded his head, ready to agree with anything to get what he needed.

The Rubber Band Man handed the bag to Michael. "Have fun," he said as he smiled and walked away.

Michael looked down at the substance in the bag and became mesmerized for a second, as if the powder inside were alive and calling to him. When he looked back up, the Rubber Band Man was gone.

Guilt gnawed at Michael all the way back to his apartment, buzzing in his ear like a persistent fly darting around his face at every turn. And the only way to quiet it was to squash it.

That was his goal as he lined the powder up on the coffee table in a series of rows and admired them for a second, like they were tiny soldiers waiting for their marching orders. Then he bowed his head, almost in reverence, uttering a silent prayer to the drug gods, and snorted deeply.

For a long moment, he was disappointed. Nothing happened. No euphoria. No wild trip. Not even the tiniest inkling of a buzz.

Fear started creeping in. Sweat beaded on his forehead. His

breathing grew erratic. *What am I going to do now?* He thought desperately. Without his fix, he'd be defenseless against the nightmares that he knew would return.

Without warning, the room suddenly spun upside down. Vertigo hit him hard, and he fell backward onto the floor, the force pinning him down and immobilizing him like he had a weighted blanket on top of his chest.

He watched as the fabric of reality whirled away from him in swirling colors. Everything melded together into one. He no longer knew up from down, left from right, then from now. Laughter bellowed from his mouth as the world around him cycled through the colors of the rainbow. It reminded him of a lesson in art class so long ago; an anagram to help remember the colors: ROYGBIV.

He called it out loud, "ROYGBIV."

Then, it became a sing-song like he was championing a fighter during a heavy-weight bout, "ROYGBIV! ROYGBIV! ROYGBIV!"

He stopped suddenly, as a low, rhythmic sound stabbed his ears, breaking through the trip he was on. It was eerily familiar, but distorted and amplified. The sound surged and surged, enveloping him in its menacing aura.

Thump-thump.

It increased in tempo as it continued to get louder.

Thump-thump. Thump-thump. Thump-thump.

Michael strained his ears for a minute before he recognized the sound as his own heartbeat. That realization triggered a flood of sudden panic coursing through him.

Thump-thump, thump-thump, thump-thump.

A surge of agony ripped through his chest as his heart threatened to burst out of his ribcage. He barely registered the sight and sound of the world around him, only the crimson drops of blood that stained his vision and filled his ears. Then he coughed and blood-tinged mucus spewed out. When he coughed again, yellow foamy-bile escaped his mouth.

He rolled to his knees and hacked his lungs out, gasping in horror when he saw a long red bloodworm wriggling on the floor amongst the expunged fluid. His eyes rolled back into his head as he fell forward beside the squirming larvae. The last thing he saw was a hand spawning from the back of the thing, waving goodbye.

Chapter 27

Jacob pounded on the steering wheel in frustration. This was the most important day of his life and he was trapped in the worst traffic jam the world had ever seen. He blasted his horn, hoping the clamor would part the sea of vehicles in front of him.

Desperation reared its ugly head as he glanced at the clock on the dash. It was already twelve-fifteen—only forty-five minutes before the ceremony was to start—and he wasn't anywhere near the church.

A quick survey of vehicles nearby found most drivers in a similar state of agitation. More than a few of them were yelling out obscenities at the unseen foe blocking their path. *Yeah, I'm sure none of you are going to be late for your own wedding,* Jacob thought bitterly.

He quickly realized he was boxed in on all sides and grew claustrophobic. He pressed the button on the door to roll his window down. The light breeze blowing in was a welcome friend and helped ease his tension just a little.

Jacob glanced at the car beside him and felt a jolt of

nostalgia. It was a 1955 Ford Fairlane Crown Victoria, a classic beauty with a red and white paint job that shone like a ruby and pearl in the sunlight. The car looked like it had just rolled off the showroom floor, a stark contrast to the modern vehicles around it. It was a vehicle out of place and out of time.

The driver and his female passenger, both dressed in garb portraying the same period as the car, nodded in unison to say, "Hello." A little red-haired boy sat in the back seat with his face pressed hard against the window. In a sea of turmoil, they appeared the only still breath.

The little boy started making funny faces at Jacob, bringing a much-needed smile to his face. He responded with a flurry of goofy faces of his own. A couple of times, the woman turned around to scold the boy, but after seeing Jacob's amusement, she let the two of them carry on.

During the exchange, Jacob had all but forgotten about the radio until the music changed abruptly and "Running with the Devil" started blasting through the speakers. He reached down quickly and turned it off.

As he turned his head back toward the car beside him, he was terrified to find that the cheerful family had vanished, replaced by monstrous beings with slender limbs and swollen heads. Their skin was a sickening shade of red, wet and shiny like raw meat. They grinned at him with wide mouths that revealed forked tongues that flicked in and out. He opened his mouth to scream, but the horror was gone in an instant.

Before he could make sense of it, the cars in front of him began to slowly move forward. For a few seconds, Jacob sat there paralyzed, staring straight ahead as he let up on the brake.

Finally, he gathered up enough courage and glanced over.

A sigh of relief issued from his lips when he saw that the family had returned to normal, although the little boy was no longer making faces at Jacob. Instead, he appeared to be sleeping with his head propped against the car window.

Traffic stopped again, and Jacob was shocked to see the mother holding a gun in her right hand. She rolled her window down and yelled over to Jacob, trying to keep her voice above the roar of the car engines. "You know, I told that little bastard twice to stop those silly games, and he wouldn't listen. Well, let's see if he disobeys me again!"

She rolled her window back up and resumed her normal posture, placing the gun on her lap.

Jacob looked back at the boy once more and saw blood streaming down from a bullet hole in his forehead. A spray of brains and blood had saturated the white leather interior of the car.

He felt a wave of panic wash over him as he shuddered violently. He backed away from the horror, desperate to escape into the passenger seat, when his foot slipped off the brake. He stomped it down with all his might and stopped the car, narrowly avoiding a collision with the car in front. His knuckles turned bone-white as he gripped the steering wheel with a savage hold, like a mongoose choking a King Cobra to death.

Somehow, the image of Terri popped into his head at that moment like a guardian angel, saving him from certain disaster. Slowly, he took a deep breath. "Calm down, Jacob," he said to himself. "It's just my exhausted brain seeing things."

He clung to the idea that it was simply his mind playing tricks on him, but it was a weak attempt to explain away the terror. When he finally gathered enough nerve, he looked at the car again and met the eyes of the family, who gazed at him with a bewildered expression, each one perfectly normal and alive.

***

"Where are we going, Mom?" Michael asked from the backseat of the car.

"Nowhere, in particular, dear. Just out for an afternoon drive."

Michael's little brother Dustin was in the seat beside him, making silly faces at the other drivers nearby. Michael chuckled softly.

"It's good to see you again, son," his dad said from the driver's seat as he bent the rear-view mirror down so he could see Michael better.

"It's good to see you too, Dad," Michael responded.

Michael turned his attention back to his brother. "Who are you making faces at?"

"Oh, just some loser in the car beside us. At first, it was fun watching him get angry because traffic was stopped. Then I thought I'd do something goofy to make him laugh."

Dustin stopped for a moment; his face twisted in thought. "Isn't that the way we're supposed to do it, Mom? First, we do something funny to make them laugh, then we turn the tables and scare the hell out of them?"

His mom's voice was full of pride as she spoke, "That's exactly right, dear."

Dustin twisted his neck with a guttural growl, his eyes burning with malice and his fangs dripping with venom. "You should be in Hell with us right now, you bastard! This is all your fault, after all!" he said.

Then he lunged at Michael.

Their mother grabbed Dustin firmly.

"Calm down, Dustin!" she said. "It's not his fault. He wasn't there when the other car hit us. He had more important things to do. After all, he was in love with his little whore-of-a-girlfriend. Besides, he's not the one we're after today, remember?"

The dead family looked out the window to the car on the right and its lone occupant.

The man was supposed to be rushing toward the best day of his life, finding rapture in the sweet embrace of his one, true love, but Michael knew instead, that this man would die a terrible and hollow death today.

Chapter 28

A moment later, traffic was moving again, this time at almost normal speed. Soon Jacob was turning off the freeway onto the exit ramp, afraid to look into his rear-view mirror.

As he exited the freeway, he glanced to his left and saw the source of their delay. He had hurled his abuse and curses at an invisible foe, only thinking of himself. Now his heart broke for the woman lying on the side of the road, encircled by paramedics. Even from a distance, he could sense the despair on the faces of the rescuers as they battled to save the victim. They shouted orders to each other, while the blinking lights from the ambulance cast a grim glow over the scene. The light reflected on the shattered glass that scattered the highway, the fragments of the little blue sports car that was wrecked beyond recognition.

He hung his head, both in shame and sorrow for the woman who was about to die.

He caught a brief flash in the back of his mind that the car was the same color as Terri's car. Did the victim have red hair too? *Of course, Terri wouldn't have any reason to be here—she lives on the other side of town.* But even as he tried to push away that thought, it still dug its claws down his spine and into the pit of his stomach.

Then, as Jacob rounded the curve of the exit ramp, the wreckage of the crash disappeared from his vision, bringing his focus once more on the task at hand: to make it to the church on time!

Jacob exhaled as he pulled into the church parking lot and glanced at the clock. Twelve forty-five.

He glanced at the rear-view mirror for a moment to fix his hair, and was terrified when he saw the Whitaker Brothers slumped in the backseat of his car with pale, lifeless faces.

"Cutting it kinda close there, aren't you, Squeezy?" Caleb hissed.

"Wasn't that your woman's car back there?" Trent taunted.

A mad cackle erupted from both boys as maggots crawled out of their rotting mouths. Jacob whirled around in his seat, but the back of the car was vacant.

With trembling hands, Jacob opened the car door and walked up the steps to the church, a feeling of dread encompassing him once more.

His dad, Henry, a short and stocky no-nonsense man, was sitting on the bench inside the foyer waiting nervously. He jumped to his feet as Jacob burst through the door. "My god, Son, it's about time you showed up!"

Jacob was about to respond but held his tongue when he heard the edge in his father's voice. Instead, he only said that there had been an accident, and kept quiet.

His best man, Alex, dashed out of the sanctuary and embraced Jacob warmly. His only true friend, besides family, he had been the pillar that had supported Jacob through all the pressure and hassle that goes into planning a wedding. His dry sense of humor was about the only thing keeping

Jacob sane.

"It's about time you showed up," Alex said. "I was afraid for a minute I'd have to step in and marry Terri for you."

"You know me, always one for a dramatic entrance," Jacob replied.

He looked around for a second. "Where's Mom?"

"She's in with the bridesmaids putting on the finishing touches," his dad said. "And before you ask, Tanya's helping Terri get ready. You know women and their pampering."

No one realized the amount of comfort that simple statement brought to Jacob.

***

Terri fought hard to conceal it, but she was paralyzed with fear. This was meant to be her special day, but she had a gnawing feeling that everything around her was about to crumble to dust.

She loved Jacob with all her heart, but this morning she'd woken up with such a sense of dread. And it was more than just wedding-day jitters. Something felt terribly wrong. Her heart pounded in her chest, her palms were cold and clammy, and her mouth was dry. She wished she could run away and hide, but she knew she couldn't. The lump in her throat grew exponentially bigger when she glanced at the clock and saw that it was almost time.

Tonya frowned as she sensed her daughter's trepidation. "Don't worry, dear," she said, trying her best to calm her down. "Everything's going to be fine. You two are perfect together."

"Thanks, Mom," Terri said. "I guess I'm just nervous I'm going to mess up my vows or something."

Tanya chuckled. "It's normal to be nervous. Just take a

deep breath and everything will be alright."

Terri wished it were that easy. She tried, but she couldn't shake the feeling.

Just as Tanya was tightening the last strap on the back of Terri's dress, Jacob's mother, Betty, peeked her head inside the room and looked at Terri for a second. "Wow! You look amazing!"

"Thank you," Terri replied with a half-hearted smile.

"It's time," Betty said.

Time for what, though? Terri thought somberly as she followed them out of the room.

***

The priest emerged through the door and beckoned the men to follow him. Jacob felt a strange calmness wash over him as he walked down the aisle with steady steps, feeling the eyes of the guests on him. The priest smiled and nodded at him as he climbed the platform and took his place.

Jacob watched with awe as the procession followed him, each one glowing in their attire. The bridesmaids shimmered in their lavender dresses, while the groomsmen looked sharp in their burgundy tuxedos. Even though he heard the soft music and the whispers of the guests, his attention was fixed on the entrance.

He waited with bated breath for Terri to appear. When she finally stepped into sight, Jacob felt his knees go weak and his breath catch in his throat. His heart, which had been surprisingly calm until then, pounded wildly. He watched her walk down the aisle with grace and radiance, her dress shimmering in the light.

Moments later, Terri was standing before him, a vision of beauty. *I'm the luckiest man in the world,* he thought to himself.

He gently lifted the satin lace veil that hid her face and was shocked to see her cheeks flushed and the hint of tears glistening in the corners of her eyes. Her expression revealed a deep-seated feeling of worry and uncertainty.

Jacob tried to console her with his own eyes, silently telling her that everything was going to be all right. He even crossed them at one point, which brought a much-needed smile to her lips. But her doubt had already worked its way into Jacob's brain as he began to wonder what kind of disaster lay ahead.

Chapter 29

The Priest, an elderly man with a long, drawn face, opened his bible on the pedestal before him and started the ceremony. "Dearly beloved, we are gathered here today..."

Michael nestled into the last pew of the church, mesmerized by the ritual. The bride and groom glowed with radiance as they faced the clergyman, both visions of grace and elegance.

As the priest uttered the first words, a silence enveloped the assembly. That's when Michael noticed that not only had the chatter ceased, but everyone had frozen in place as well.

The alcove behind the priest was a large archway stretching twenty feet up and spanned the width of the altar where the priest was speaking. Above the arch was a large stained-glass window depicting the beheading of John the Baptist. Michael thought it odd that a gruesome image like this would be found in such a holy place.

A long arm, its flesh gray and mottled, suddenly reached up from the floor below the archway and stretched toward the bloody sword depicted in the glass. With gnarled claws, it grabbed the hilt of the weapon, bringing it alive into the present world. As the arm brought the sword down and pointed it at Michael, three more sets of claws extended from the darkness and pulled the rest of the beast forward from the shadows, revealing itself. And it was an abomination, pure and evil.

The creature overshadowed the priest, a dark, wet horror. A blank sheet of flesh hid its eyes, but it saw everything. Its mouth split open, spitting out a cascade of razor blades, and a deafening howl burst from the demon. As it stalked closer, it showed its full horror. Its human torso abruptly morphed into a segmented hell with endless barbed legs on both sides.

The priest extended his arms as if he were presenting the monster to the congregation. He cleared his throat as his form changed to that of Belial and continued, "If anyone present finds a reason these two should not be wed," he looked right at Michael, "let them speak now and die!"

He pointed at Michael. And the demon gave a loud shriek before it swept forward, descending on him with lightning speed.

Michael quickly dodged to his right to avoid the first attack, but the thing was too fast. It hit him across the chest with a strong backhand that sent him flying across the pew and crashing to the floor. Michael rolled over and looked up just as the demon drove the point of the sword through his chest.

***

Jacob was so focused on Terri's face that he barely heard the priest as he started speaking. The words were like echoes in his mind as he stood there detached from the world around him. At this moment, the only thing that seemed real was the woman standing before him.

Luckily, he had rehearsed his lines about a thousand times and could issue them automatically from his brain right on cue. Terri's face brightened as the ceremony started, and her voice was like that of an angel as she replied with her own vows.

When the time came to put the ring on her finger. Jacob turned to Alex. The customary fumbling around in the pockets followed before he smiled and handed the ring over to Jacob. The stone sparkled as if the light of the sun were shining through.

Jacob turned back to Terri and saw a playful, devious look on her face. He lifted her hand, and just as he was about to push the ring onto her finger, the stone changed to blood red before swirling to pitch black. He tried to pull his hand back, but Terri thrust her finger forward, locking the ring in place. Four tiny pins with needle-sharp points extended from the stone and embedded themselves in Terri's flesh.

She let out a banshee scream, and Jacob watched in horror as her face transformed into something terrifying. Her eyes roared like fire, with the wide-eyed look of a caged animal glowing from them. Her teeth had become huge fangs behind her ruby red lips. Even her hair had changed to darkest midnight.

Jacob tried to stumble backward, but Terri grabbed him and held him tight. Alex came up behind him, patted him on the shoulder like an old school buddy, and whispered in his ear, "Don't worry, Buddy. It'll all be over soon."

A deep, sinister laugh erupted from the priest laugh. His voice was triumphant as he spoke. "You may now kiss the bride!"

Terri embraced Jacob even tighter, but instead of bringing her lips to his, she rammed her sharp fangs down hard on his neck. Jacob cried out as he felt the deadly daggers rip into his flesh and the blood flow.

A roar of cheers flew up from the congregation that shook the very foundation of the church. The room began to spin as Jacob teetered on the narrow ledge between life and death. Then everything went dark.

***

Suddenly, Jacob was standing before the priest once more. The man looked at him with a deep-rooted fear on his face and made the sign of the cross with trembling hands before speaking, "Dearly beloved, we are gathered here today..."

Jacob's mind was spinning. *The ceremony hasn't even started!*

He looked over at Terri and saw the same look of fear on her face. She grabbed his hand and squeezed it tightly, then she turned toward the priest, "I'm sorry, Father, but we can't continue."

Her voice was trembling. "I don't know what's going on right now, but I can't marry this man. Something's telling me it's all wrong."

The priest urged her to take a deep breath. "Follow your heart, child. This man loves you deeply, and I know you feel the same for him. Fight the force that is tormenting your soul right now!"

A devilish look came over Terri's face for a brief second and her voice became deep and powerful, "Pathetic fool! You have no idea what forces you're talking about! Don't worry. Soon enough, the whole world will feel my wrath!"

The priest stumbled backward and fell, tripping over the hem of his robes. Terri turned and ran down the aisle toward the exit, leaving a heartbroken man standing at the altar in disbelief.

After the initial shock slowly subsided, Jacob crumpled to the floor, weeping bitterly. His life had instantly exploded into a million pieces. He was a hollow shell of man, with no hope to ever to mend his shattered heart.

After a few minutes, the audience rose and exited the sanctuary, most of them shaking their heads in disbelief while offering a silent prayer. Soon, only Jacob, his parents, and Alex were left in the vast room.

They all sat there for a long time, trying to console Jacob, but he remained silent. Finally, when the tears dried up, Jacob looked at his mother questioningly. "I don't understand? What just happened? I thought she loved me?"

Betty was speechless. A sharp pang of helplessness pierced her heart as she watched her child writhe in agony. She was powerless to take away his pain. Therefore, she did the only thing she could do—she wrapped him in her arms and squeezed him tight.

"Why don't I see if I can find Terri? Maybe I can talk to her," Alex offered.

Jacob just nodded absently.

After Alex left, Jacob stood up slowly. His knees were shaky under his weight for a second, but then he steadied himself.

"I think I'm going to go for a drive; try to sort things out in my head," he said. "I'll call you later tonight so we can talk."

In the back of his mind, Jacob had a feeling that he wouldn't be making that call.

Slowly, he made his way up the same aisle that he had so excitedly walked down a short time ago. He exited through the hallway and out the side door that led to the parking lot.

Jacob stumbled toward his vehicle, his head throbbing with pain and grief. He felt a surge of terror as he looked up and saw a horrific sight: severed limbs and organs tied to black ribbons that dripped with blood adorning his car like a twisted wedding cake. On the back window, someone had carved 'Just Buried' with a sharp knife, leaving deep scratches on the glass.

He gave a loud gasp, and in a flash, everything vanished to reveal the normal sight of balloons and tin cans attached to the car, bouncing and rattling in the wind, along with the 'Just Married' sign that sparkled on the rear window

Jacob collapsed again. This time, a gut-wrenching sickness swept over him and he fell forward, spewing onto the pavement. The heaving became so intense that he felt a sharp pain in his chest, like something had burst inside him.

After the nausea faded, he got up weakly and reached for the door handle, searching the parking lot. His eyes sparkled with hope for a fleeting moment when he saw a blue sports car that resembled Terri's car. Hope crumbled quickly, however, when a stranger opened the door and got in.

Jacob sat in his car for a long minute, just staring ahead blankly. He started to cry again, but stopped himself.

He heard Caleb's voice behind him again, "Awe! Is Squeezy Wheezy sad? Boo-hoo!"

"Go ahead. Start crying like a little girl, you fat fuck!" Trent added.

Their hideous laughter filled the car.

Jacob cringed in fear, but refused to look in the rear-view mirror.

Then he heard Terri's voice beside him. "Did you really think it would work out between us, Jacob? I mean, look at you! You're a fucking mess!"

Jacob turned his head slowly toward Terri with misty eyes. "I thought we were happy together? I thought you loved me?"

Terrie's eyes turned dangerous. "Well, you were wrong. It

took me a minute, but I finally realized a life with you would lead me nowhere. I can't believe I wasted a year of my life with you."

His lips quivered. "Why are you saying such horrible things?"

"Because it's the truth. Looking back, it probably would've been better if you'd just died there on the sidewalk."

A torrent of tears fell from Jacob's eyes.

"See how pathetic you are, Jacob?" Terri said. "I should just put you out of your misery right here."

Terri lunged for Jacob, swiping at him with sharp claws.

Jacob put his arm up to block the attack and found himself alone once more in the vehicle. A long, soulful cry poured out of him. Finally, he turned the car on and decided that he was just going to drive...somewhere.

He ended up driving past Terri's house just to see if her car was in the driveway. He knew it wouldn't be, but he had to check. Like his heart at that moment, her house was dark and empty. Then Jacob hit the gas and sped away.

Chapter 30

"Come out, come out, wherever you are," Belial called out. "I know you're hiding in here. I can feel you close. I can smell your fear."

Michael curled himself into a ball, shivering in the damp, pitch-black closet, not daring to open his eyes. He prayed fervently for a miracle, for a way out of this nightmare, but his prayers fell on deaf ears. He was trapped in a Hell-scape that had no end.

A second later, the door exploded outward and the eyes of Belial glared at him through the darkness. "Ah, there you. I see you haven't learned your lesson yet."

Belial snatched Michael by his hair, ripping it from his scalp as he dragged him over the jagged planks that pierced his flesh with splinters. He wrapped his other hand around his throat and hoisted him up in the air, bringing him close enough to feel his hot breath on his face. "Since you like to watch so much, why don't we see how our buddy, Jacob, is doing?"

Jacob's car was a prison of agony. Every station he switched to was a cruel reminder of his shattered love. The songs that once made him smile now stabbed him in the chest. He desperately hit the button, searching for an escape from the nightmare. At last, he found a metal station and turned up the volume to the max. He let the furious music fill his ears, hoping to silence the screams of his heart.

His foot became heavy as he pressed on the accelerator with all his might. He was driving parallel to the large river that ran through the center of the city. He knew immediately what he needed to do. The muscles in Jacob's arms tightened as he braced himself in his seat, and when the road turned sharply to his left, he simply continued straight.

***

Michael was shocked to see that they were standing on top of the water in the middle of a river.

"What's the matter?" Belial asked. "Did you think your Jesus was the only one who could walk on water?"

He chuckled softly. "It should be any second now. Just keep your eyes on the riverbank ahead."

The speeding car flipped up over the protective guardrail and tumbled through the air. It sailed fifty or sixty yards before landing with a hard thud on top of the swiftly moving water. The force of the impact brought Jacob to the brink of unconsciousness. His body was broken and bleeding, and a few seconds later, the water rushed into his lungs as it carried the car down into its black depths.

"I give it a 9.5," Belial said as if he were a judge at a sporting event. "The landing could've made a bigger splash, but overall, it was quite impressive, don't you think?"

Belial turned to Michael. "Now it's your turn, dick-wad. You've interfered with my plans enough. Time for you to die!"

Belial was gone in a flash, and Michael felt a sudden drop. He plunged into the water with a splash, feeling a heavy force drag him down. He thrashed his arms wildly, trying to find a way up, but the water had become a bottomless abyss.

Michael felt his life slipping away as he ran out of air. He struggled to reach the surface, praying for a miracle, but something snatched him with a ruthless grip. He looked down in panic as a grotesque face rose out of the murk. It had huge yellow eyes that gleamed at him with evil. It pulled him deeper into the water with its razor-sharp claws. Then its powerful jaws clamped down hard on Michael's leg.

As soon as he opened his mouth in an underwater scream, water rushed in and filled his lungs. Seconds later, he was sinking to join Jacob in his watery grave.

Chapter 31

A violent cough went through Michael, shaking him from the trance that had taken hold of him. In terror, he looked around and realized he was lying on the floor of his apartment. No signs of his drug-induced trip were found—no slimy residue of the bloodworm left behind; not a tiny speck of Maelstrom on the carpet; not even the mercury-laced taste that normally lingered in the back of his throat after the drugs had worn off.

It was a mixture of terror and relief that found its way into the fabric of Michael's soul. Relief that none of the horrific events he had witnessed were real, and terrified that he was coming unglued. He could feel his sanity slipping away, moment by moment, inch by inch.

Michael curled up tight on the living room floor, fighting to hide back a wave of tears, and suddenly felt a sharp pain in his right leg. He reached down and rolled his pant leg up. What he saw frightened him beyond belief. A row of bite marks in a circular pattern—one that matched the sea creature in his dream—covered the back of his calf.

The wound was gaping and oozing with black puss. The skin around the edges of the wound turned black, and the blackness begins to climb up his leg, enveloping him. Soon, the infection spread to his stomach, and then his chest. Michael's body convulsed violently under the onslaught. Then everything went dark.

Michael was only dimly aware of a soft knocking on his front door. The sound was a gentle rapping that seemed to be from a thousand miles away. After a couple of minutes, it stopped. Then he drifted back into nothingness.

It wasn't until he felt his body rocking back and forth that his senses returned. Slowly, he found the strength to open his eyes and saw a blurry image standing over him. Eventually, his vision sharpened, and he realized it was Mary straddling him, shaking him vigorously.

Her words were desperate and pleading, "Michael, please wake up!"

After a few seconds, he found the strength to sit up. He looked at her, his own red and swollen eyes matching hers, and said quietly, "It happened again."

An avalanche of images assaulted Michael's mind. He felt the water choke his lungs as he plunged to the cold abyss of the river; felt the creature tear his leg with its jaws; felt the demon stab his heart with its blade. All of that was nothing compared to seeing Mary betray him in his dream. That broke him inside.

Michael collapsed in a heap of tears and Mary wrapped her arms around him, pouring her soul into his broken one, hoping to mend the cracks that the darkness had left behind. She loved him more than anything, that was never in doubt. But she doubted if she could survive in this hellish nightmare that had become their reality.

"Come on, Michael," she finally said. "We're leaving

now."

Michael's voice broke into a thousand pieces of pain as he spoke. "Where are we going?"

"We're going to figure this out," Mary said.

Within a few minutes, they were inside Mary's car, heading for the hospital. Almost as if she was reading his mind, Mary said, "I know we don't have an appointment, but I'm hoping that if we explain the situation, someone will see us."

Michael didn't share the same optimism. To him, the idea of hope had disappeared a long time ago. Now he had resigned himself to the fact that he was doomed to live the rest of his life in mental and emotional torment.

As soon as Michael saw the hospital, a wave of anxiety coursed through him. "Do we have to go in there? Isn't there somewhere else we can go for help?"

Mary replied, "Listen, Michael, there's nothing to be afraid of. I'm here with you. We'll get through whatever the hell this is together. Okay?"

"Yeah, unless they throw me in the fucking psych ward!"

"Don't talk like that."

Michael tried to look brave as they got out of the car. He glanced around nervously as they approached the steps to the entrance. A loud gasp flew out of him when he saw Julie, Harold, and Jacob standing near the door. All of them looked very dead. Julie's neck was bent at an unnatural angle, half of Harold's face was blown off, and Jacob's skin was mottled blue with water dripping from it in unnatural puddles.

Mary asked nervously, "What is it? What's wrong?

The apparitions disappeared suddenly, leaving Michael shaken. "I just thought I saw something," he said quickly.

Mary grabbed Michael's hand and squeezed it tight as they walked inside. She walked up to the reception desk with

Michael walking behind her, his head hung down low.

The receptionist, an older woman in her forties, was busy typing on a keyboard while looking at a computer monitor.

"Excuse me," Mary interrupted, "I need to see if we can get my boyfriend some help."

The woman stopped her typing and looked over toward Mary, and then at Michael. "The emergency entrance is on the west side of the building," she said coldly.

"It's not really an emergency, but he desperately needs help."

The receptionist paused for a second before giving in, sighing, "What seems to be the problem?"

"He's having trouble sleeping. He has nightmares pretty much every night. And some of them have gotten really violent. I'm afraid he's going to hurt himself accidentally."

The woman picked up the phone and held it loosely in her hand for a second. "Okay. Give me a minute and I'll see what I can do. Do you have insurance?"

Mary gave the lady a wounded look.

The receptionist sighed again, mumbling 'Why am I not surprised,' as she dialed the phone. After talking for a minute, she hung up. "One of our physicians will be out shortly to talk to you. You can have a seat in the waiting area."

Mary grabbed Michael's hand again as they walked over to the waiting area.

Michael's knee bounced up and down as he sat nervously on one of the chairs, picking at his fingernails. Mary put her hand on his thigh to calm him down.

"I'm here for you, Michael," she said. "It's going to be okay."

Michael looked at Mary worriedly, but didn't say anything. Across from him, unknown to her, sat the trio of apparitions again. Julie, Harold, and Jacob all regarding Michael coldly. He kept his head down low and picked at his fingers to avoid looking at them.

A minute later, Dr. Samuel, a man with blond hair wearing a white overcoat, with a distinctive hippie vibe, entered the waiting area. He looked sternly toward the three spirits and they instantly disappeared.

The doctor extended his hand in greeting. "Hi, I'm Dr. Samuel," he said eagerly.

Michael took his offering and felt his firm, reassuring grip. He couldn't help but think he had seen this man somewhere before.

"Thank you for seeing us without an appointment," Mary said.

The doctor looked at Mary. "You're quite welcome. After all, that's why we're here—to help those in need."

He turned to look squarely at Michael, "I've been told you've had a problem sleeping lately—recurring dreams and nightmares?"

Michael replied with a nod. *If only it were that simple.*

Dr. Samuel looked deeply into Michael's eyes. "The nightmares only have power over you if you give them strength. Do not give in to the evil and it will fall away. Instead of fearing your dreams, embrace them and learn from them. Once you know where they stem from, you can defeat them."

Those words struck a chord in Michael, and suddenly he remembered the security guard from a previous dream. The message was almost identical, as was the messenger.

The doctor leaned forward and whispered to Michael, "He fears you. He knows you have the power to destroy everything he's worked for and is scared. And well, he should be."

He turned and led them down a long corridor, which ended abruptly at a single door. For a second, a lump formed in Michael's throat as he remembered the door from his dreams and the horror that had waited beyond. However, unlike that door, this one had Dr. Samuel stenciled on it in big black letters.

Dr. Samuel guided them into a room that buzzed with scientific activity. A dark desk and a dusty bookcase contrasted with the gleaming medical devices that filled the space. Cabinets, counters, and monitors flashed with colorful lights and data. A stark examination bed loomed in the center, surrounded by a halo of lamps.

After Dr. Samuel had prepared the bed and Michael was comfortable, he said in a soothing voice, "Now I want you to lie back and relax, Michael. Let the sleep come over you, but this time when the dreams come—and they will—do not fear them. Be strong and observe; watch and learn. Do not give your power to this evil."

Michael closed his eyes as instructed. Sleep overtook his weary mind almost immediately. And the Dream Master was waiting for him as expected.

Chapter 32

Nazareth, 43 A.D., in the gloomy shadows of a ramshackle stable far from the city's bustling center, Isabel's shriek shattered the silence as another spasm of agony wracked her body. Her ebony tresses stuck to her face, soaked in sweat that cascaded down her brow.

Joseph's eyes were oceans of love and terror, drowning her in their depths. He clutched his wife's hand like a lifeline, as he kneeled on the cold floor beside her.

On the other side of Isabel sat the angel Gloriana, a vision of beauty, radiating. She held Isabel's other hand and was praying softly, while a nursemaid was on her knees between Isabel's legs, helping her with the delivery.

"You're almost there, Isabel." Joseph said earnestly. "Just a few more minutes."

Joseph's brother, Simon, suddenly burst into the stable out of breath and visibly shaken. "Is the child here yet?"

"Almost, Brother."

"I pray that it's soon, then, for I fear the devil is at our heels."

"In what form?"

"I saw several of Pilot's men traveling this direction. But that's not all. They had something evil with them. I could feel it."

Joseph turned to Isabel, "Then we must not tarry. Isabel, my sweet, we don't have much time. You must push with all of your might."

Isabel's tears blurred her vision as she locked eyes with Joseph. His eyes were wild and desperate, pleading with her. She bit her lip and nodded before summoning all her courage. Then she pushed with a guttural roar. A heartbeat later, a faint cry broke the silence, making them gasp with relief.

"Quickly, give the baby to me," Gloriana said to the nursemaid after she had wrapped her in linen.

Gloriana cuddled the baby in her arms and exhaled softly on her, murmuring a few words that sparkled in the air. A radiant glow embraced the newborn for a brief instant and then faded.

"Can I hold her, if only for a moment before she's gone," Isabel asked weakly.

Gloriana softly nestled the baby onto Isabel's breast. Gentle tears streamed down Isabel's face as she beheld the child's innocent eyes.

"My sweet angel. I pray that you go on to accomplish great things."

A chorus of howls sounded in the distance, and Joseph looked nervously at Simon.

"Are you ready?" Joseph asked.

Simon nodded.

Joseph took the baby from Isabel and handed her to him. "Go, now, with God's speed! Keep her safe."

Simon replied, "I will protect her as if the world depended

on it."

"It does," Joseph said.

Simon rushed out of the stable with the baby tightly in his arms.

Gloriana leaned down at Isabel, who trembled at the verge of life and death, holding the delicate silver thread before it slipped. "You have done well, Isabel," she said with a warm and sad voice. "Be at peace now."

She put her hand on Isabel's forehead and a soft gasp escaped her lips as the final breath of life floated away and she died.

Tears streamed down Joseph's eyes as he watched his beloved's light extinguished.

Gloriana said, "Take comfort and know that her sacrifice will one day save the world." Then she left, leaving Joseph to mourn alone.

Suddenly, a massive dire wolf crashed into the stable, followed by a Roman centurion. The soldier drew his sword and pressed it against Joseph's neck. "Where is the child?" he snarled.

Joseph spat at the man. "I'll tell you nothing, Roman pig!"

"We shall see about that."

A second later, the chief of the Centurion army, Cassius, a brawny and arrogant man, barged into the stable with his chest swollen and a second black dire wolf at his flank.

"Cassius! I thought I smelled your foul stench nearby," Joseph said.

Cassius chuckled. "Brave words coming from a coward hiding in a stable out in the middle of nowhere."

He looked over at Isabel's body lying in a pool of blood. "Did you feel helpless as you watched your wife die, knowing that if you had obeyed Pilot's decree, she'd still be with you now?"

"Do not try to trick me with your words, Cassius! We both know that Pilot's so-called decree placed an immediate death sentence on my unborn child."

"Only those who violated his law were in danger of feeling his wrath. Those that complied had nothing to fear."

"Pilot thinks himself above God."

Cassius shrugged. "Pilot can think whatever he wants to think. He rules this land. Now, about that child of yours you spoke about? Where might the infant be at this moment?"

"Like I told your other murderous scum here," Joseph said defiantly, "I go to my grave knowing that, in the end, evil shall be defeated."

Cassius gave a signal to the centurion, who slammed the hilt of his sword on the back of Joseph's head. Joseph let out a cry and then collapsed, motionless.

***

A throbbing sensation in his head brought Joseph back to reality. He blinked and tried to focus his vision. He was staring at the sky, but it was distorted and twisted. A cold sweat stood on his forehead as he tried to scream, but his throat was dry and sore. He was trapped in a hellish contraption, tied upside down to a cross outside the stable where he had sought refuge. A few feet in front of him, the faces of the centurion soldiers mocked and taunted him. He smelled the stench of his own blood, dripping from his wounds. Across from him were tied two other men, caught in the same torment.

"Glad you could finally join us again, Joseph of Galilee," Cassius said. "As you can see, the situation has gotten much more serious. I'm going to give you one last chance. Where is the child?"

The two men shook in fear as the wolves inched closer to their throats, each one pleading desperately for their lives.

Joseph looked at the men and cried bitterly, "I can't. I just can't. I'm sorry."

"Well, that was a wasted effort!" Cassius exclaimed. He barked a sharp command, and the two wolves sprang forward and ripped into the men's throats, killing them quickly in a gruesome display that turned the ground a deep shade of red in seconds.

The large, black, dire wolf walked slowly up to Joseph, baring its teeth. "Last chance," Cassius said.

Joseph hung there silent, his jaw clenched defiantly, as he held his secret silent in the last moments of his life.

"Goodbye, Joseph," Cassius said. "May your soul rot in Hell!"

Joseph replied, "Not likely. Although, I'm sure there's already a room reserved there for you and your ilk."

Cassius growled at Joseph angrily and then barked another command that sent the last wolf lunging forward. Joseph cried out for a brief second before his voice was cut short.

***

Simon felt the horse's muscles strain under him as they raced frantically through the dark woods. He dug his heels into the steed's flanks, hoping to outrun the evil that was gaining on them, the blood-curdling howls of the beasts snapping at his heels. He clutched the baby tighter to his chest, whispering words of comfort and protection as her tiny heart beat against his own. He had sworn to keep her safe, and he would die before he let the monsters take her from him.

The flash of azure ahead was a beacon of hope, as the forest gave way to the serene waters of the Sea of Galilee.

Simon urged his horse on even harder, knowing it was already pushed to its limit. He looked back and gasped. The dire wolves were monstrous figures in the dark, evil radiating from them with such intensity that he felt a small tremor flow through his steed as its heart stuttered for a second. Alongside them, the hooves of the centurion's steeds thundered on the ground like drums that rattled his bones.

The horse burst out of the forest into the clearing and raced toward the nearest shore, where a man in a black cloak stood beside a small boat. The man caught sight of Simon and quickly shoved the boat into the water and jumped inside.

"Simon, hurry up!" the man shouted. "They're coming!"

Simon slammed his horse to a halt at the water's edge and jumped off, racing frantically toward the boat with the baby in his arms. He was almost there when two colossal dire wolves lunged toward him, followed by Cassius and a squad of Centurion soldiers.

With the beasts snapping at his heels, Simon quickly handed the baby to the cloaked man. "Guard her with your life."

"Indeed, I shall," the man said as he placed the baby at his feet and started rowing the boat out on the water feverishly.

The dire wolves leaped into the water after the boat, howling and snapping viciously, even as a fierce squall exploded around them. Thunder and lightning split the sky, and soon the man vanished into the storm's rage. Still, the beasts continued their pursuit until the power of the sea dragged them downward to their watery graves.

Simon fell to his knees in the water exhausted, as Cassius trotted toward him with his sword drawn. "This is the end for you, Simon. You do realize that you'll be crucified for your crimes against the State just as your accursed brother was?"

Simon looked at him with a cryptic smile, "I go to my death willingly then, knowing that evil was thwarted this day."

"Well then," Cassius said, "if you're so eager to join your brother, then let's not waste another minute.

Cassius nodded at two of the centurions, who snatched Simon from the water and held him up before the general. "I'll give you one last chance to clear your conscious before you die like the traitor that you are. What was the significance of the child, and what was the boatman's destination?"

Simon laughed, "You speak in the past as if the child were deceased and you have won, Cassius. Nothing could be further from the truth. My conscious is clear before God, and as I face the end of my mortal life knowing that I have fulfilled my duties, that is all that matters."

A loud roar erupted from Cassius as he rammed his sword deep into Simon's stomach. A river of blood poured into the sea as he pulled the blade out. Simon dropped to his knees, teetering on the brink of death.

Cassius nodded to the centurions, who dragged Simon from the water up the sandy bank toward the horses gathered there. Each arm and leg was tied to the flank of one of the powerful steeds. A sharp thwack to the flanks of the animals sent them spurring forward in different directions. Howls and cries of agony flew from Simon as he was pulled limb from limb before he finally succumbed to his fate.

One of the other centurions trotted up to join Cassius. "What shall we tell Pilot about the child?" he asked.

Cassius looked out at the waters for a moment and frowned. "We'll simply tell him the child is dead. Nothing could survive that tempest, least of all a helpless newborn."

***

Michael convulsed on the bed, shivering and jerking his head in agony, while Mary stared at him, her eyes wide with fear and her lips trembling. "Is he okay?" she asked worriedly.

Dr. Samuel examined the monitors next to the bed with a concerned eye, measuring Michael's heartbeat and blood pressure. He adjusted the filter on the overhead light, brightening and softening the color. After a nerve-wracking minute, Michael eased his breathing. "I think he's okay, for now." Dr. Samuel replied.

"You think? What the fuck do you mean, you think?"

"Stay strong, Mary. Michael has to learn to fight his own demons. Once he does that, he can free himself of his pain."

Mary's heart slowed down its frantic pounding just a little as she stared at Michael's motionless form on the bed, his limbs still occasionally twitching, while tears gathered behind a fragile wall in her eyes, ready to burst at any second.

Chapter 33

Freddie Smith.

The name used to mean something. Not anymore.

It once conjured up images of a superstar—an athlete of unparalleled skill in all his glory. Four touchdowns, one-hundred sixty-five yards rushing for the Bears against Dallas. It was the defining game of his career, a moment that should've propelled him toward greatness. Dreams of riches and glory danced in his head like Vegas showgirls taunting him with their sinful charms. Then, the unthinkable happened, and it all came crashing down.

Freddie followed in the footsteps of countless champions and dreamers before him, and he vowed to surpass them all. He had savored a moment of triumph that ignited a fire in his soul. With a fierce passion, he trained day and night, breaking his own limits and striving for greatness, determined to lead himself and his team to glory.

But the price of chasing a dream with such intensity is that you can lose sight of everything else—those who care for you, those who support you, and especially those who love you. It was a bitter truth he would face soon enough.

Finally, after OTA's and mini-camps were over, training camp started, signaling the beginning of a new season. Freddie came to camp in the best shape of his life, ready to bring his team to the pinnacle of the football world.

Two weeks prior, the Bears had signed their prized rookie catch, Marcus Jackson. He was a monster, and when he hit someone, they felt it. The plan was that he would turn their defense into a juggernaut. Freddie knew if that happened, along with their already explosive offense, they would be unstoppable.

Then, in a flash, two weeks into training camp, the unspeakable happened and Freddie's life was ruined forever. He ripped his knees apart in a gruesome accident during a scrimmage, cruelly ending his short-lived three-year career.

Sure, he had tried to come back. For many long months after re-constructive surgery, Freddie had gone through strenuous physical rehab and therapy, learning how to walk all over again. In time, almost full range of motion returned. But in the NFL almost doesn't cut it. His speed was nowhere near what it was before the accident, and he could no longer make the necessary cut-backs to be an effective running back. So, barely after it had begun, Freddie's dream of stardom faded into oblivion.

Freddie took another deep gulp of his beer. The playoffs were the hardest; watching other players pour their hearts on the field as they battled to seize the trophy that should've been his. Now all he could do was watch from his ragged couch in his shabby little apartment with its cheap furniture and reminisce about how it used to be.

Of course, Freddie was the ultimate armchair quarterback, sitting about a foot from his small TV, yelling at the refs and players as if they could hear him.

Finally, the whistle blew for half-time, and Freddie threw his hands up in disgust. The Bears were losing seventeen to ten and had a chance to tie it on the last play of the half, but the pass into the end zone had been wide. The receiver had gotten both hands on it, but hadn't been able to reel it in.

"Oh, my god!" Freddie exclaimed loudly. "How could you drop that pass? It was right in your hands! I'd have caught that easily."

The player looked squarely at the camera as he was about to enter the tunnel leading to the locker room and addressed Freddie directly, sending a deep chill down his spine. "But you're not here right now, are you, old man? Instead, you sit at home wallowing in self-pity, living off welfare and food stamps, while the rest of the hard-working Americans slave day after day to earn a living."

Then the player turned and disappeared down the tunnel.

As Freddie leaped off the couch in panic, agony ripped through his legs and he plummeted to the floor, smashing into the coffee table as he fell. After lying on there for a few minutes, howling in pain, he finally crawled his way back to the couch and hoisted himself up. After a torturous minute, he grabbed his cane, which had become a part of his body, much like an extra limb, and hobbled toward the bathroom.

The light flickered on and off when Freddie flipped the switch on the wall. A loud curse and a firm pounding on the wall steadied the light. "Piece-of-shit apartment!" he spat.

Freddie staggered over to the sink and gazed into the mirror. A wide cut had split open above his right eye, which was already bulging, and a thick stream of blood was dripping down his cheek. He snatched a washcloth hanging on the wall next to him and ran it under the faucet. The cold water felt soothing as he pressed the cloth onto the wound. Then he held it there for a moment as he looked into the mirror.

"My god, Freddie," he said to the image staring back at him. "You look like shit! You used to have it all, man. Now, look at you!"

Freddie dwelled on the past as he stared at the mirror. Indeed, at one time, he did have it all—a lavish house, flashy cars, a gorgeous wife, a darling baby girl. Unfortunately, his many treasures had not included a crystal ball.

It didn't take long after the accident for the collection agencies to call. Sure, Freddie had received a nice signing bonus to go along with his generous salary. And like most young adults who had grown up in an impoverished household, he was quick to spend, but slow to save. He had squandered away his riches on things that would give him immediate pleasure instead of investing it wisely. His plan was to enjoy his greatness first, and then worry about his future later.

The future came a lot sooner than expected.

It happened in an instant. The play only lasted a few seconds, but the aftermath shattered Freddie's life forever. He dashed back to his left and spun away from a tackler when another defender gripped him low around the ankles. As he was falling forward, Marcus smashed him hard in the chest, sending his body flying backward. The force of the other defender on his legs was too much, and Freddie shrieked in pain as he felt the tendons and ligaments in both knees tear apart.

When Freddie woke up later, he was horrified to find himself in a hospital bed with both legs supported in a massive sling. His mind raced as panic overtook him.

His wife, Sharee, grabbed his hand and held it tight, trying to calm him down from the chair beside the bed. Her eyes were tinged red and swollen from crying. "Shh. I'm here,

Freddie," she said in a hushed tone. "Everything's going to be okay."

Freddie stared at his legs in disbelief for a moment and then turned to his wife, his lips quivering. "What happened to my legs?"

When the doctor walked in, a cloud of apprehension followed him that drifted around the room before it settled over Freddie. "Freddie, it's good to see you're awake," he said.

Desperation shone in Freddie's eyes. "How bad is it, Doc?"

The doctor remained silent for a moment, either trying to find a delicate way to present the situation to Freddie, or he secretly enjoyed sadistically torturing people. "I'm going to give it to you straight, Son," he finally said. "Only a small percentage of patients with injuries as severe as yours ever recover completely. Most of them walk with a severe limp for the rest of their lives."

Freddie's eyes grew misty as his mind raced. "You've got to do your best, Doc. Football is my life. Without it, I don't know what I'll do?"

The doctor replied, "It'll take a miracle for you to ever play football again. Surgery is scheduled for tomorrow morning. We'll know more after."

The doctor turned to leave the room. Then he saw the look of desperation on Freddie's face and said words he shouldn't have; words that gave Freddie a false sense of hope: "But I've been in this business long enough to never count out a miracle."

After he left, Freddie looked at Sharee with sheer terror in his eyes. "What are we gonna do?"

"We'll get through this, Freddie," Sharee answered. "Just like every other thing that's come up in the past. You're strong. If anybody can come out of something like this on top, it's you."

Freddie squeezed her hand lightly. "I hope so," he said sadly. He looked at his legs propped up in the air like they were a display in a drugstore window and started crying.

***

A series of scratching noises woke Freddie sometime later. He looked around in panic. At first, the sound echoed around the room, but then, as he focused his senses, he triangulated it to his legs. He looked down toward his limbs, which were encased in thick plaster casts.

Freddie suddenly cried out as he felt a swarm of stings converge on his extremities, then watched in horror as both casts started to crack and split open. An instant later, hordes of black spiders poured out of the casings and instantly swarmed over him. He tried to scream, but his voice was suffocated by the onslaught.

Chapter 34

Freddie stared at himself in the mirror through sad eyes. The light flickered on the bathroom wall again, bringing Freddie out of his trance and back to the present. The pounding on the wall ritual did the trick once more.

The water from the faucet turned red as Freddie ran the washcloth under it. After dabbing at his wound again, he placed his hands on both sides of the sink and sighed.

***

The surgeries took a combined twelve hours, with the doctors and nurses working tirelessly to mend Freddie's broken body, and hopefully, with it, his broken dream.

During the night, he woke up screaming. Quickly, a nurse rushed in and administered a dose of pain medication through his IV, and within seconds, he was asleep again. He would come to rely heavily on this pain medication.

Freddie woke up, groggy from the bevy of medications, just as the doctor came into his room. His legs were now wrapped in thick casts, the sight of which brought his nightmare rocketing back to him and sent a shudder coursing through his spine.

The doctor said, "While it's still too early to tell, I would consider the operation a success. We repaired all the damage to your right knee, and are confident that it should return to full strength. Your left knee, however, had sustained far worse damage. With hard work, I'd estimate a return to ninety percent range of motion."

Freddie got agitated. "What about football? How long before I can get back on the field?"

The doctor shook his head, "In my professional opinion, I don't think that's a possibility. Even if you were to make a comeback, another injury would likely cause irreparable damage."

Tears cascaded down Freddie's face. "You don't get it, Doc! Football is all I know! How am I gonna take care of my family?"

Sharee grabbed Freddie's hand and looked into his eyes. "We're gonna figure this out, okay? We'll get through this."

The doctor turned and walked toward the door, but stopped on his way out. "I'm sorry. We've done all we can."

The words hit him like a freight train. What was he going to do? How was he going to survive? He had skated through college on his football scholarship, doing just enough to pass his classes, but not enough to gain any real-world knowledge or experience. Football had been his whole life. He wasn't trained to do anything else. How would his family be able to live?

Sharee held him tight as he cried into her shoulder, telling him that everything was going to be all right, while inside she was just as scared as he was.

Nearly three weeks later, Freddie was released from the

hospital and returned home to find that his teammates had overrun his house. Marcus Jackson, the man responsible for the end of Freddie's career, was the first one to approach Freddie.

"I'm so sorry, man," he said in a guilt-ridden voice. "I didn't mean for nothing like this to happen. I just got caught up in the play."

Marcus had quickly become one of Freddie's best friends on the team, and it hurt Freddie to see him tormented emotionally like this. "It's not your fault, man. It was just one of those freak accidents you hear about."

They embraced again for a second, and when they pulled away, a spark of electricity passed between their fingers.

Freddie looked at Marcus in shock, who responded with a sly smile. Marcus' eyes turned pitch black and his face grew long and sinister. "What's the matter, Freddie? You had everything you always wanted. Well, now you get everything you deserved."

A surge of terror overcame Freddie as he clutched his wheelchair. He scanned the room with wide eyes and saw the grotesque forms of his former teammates. They had been twisted and mutated into horrific creatures that barely resembled humans.

Freddie cried out in fear, but when he looked again, Marcus and his teammates had turned back to normal and everyone in the room was staring at him.

"What's wrong, Hun?" Sharee asked worriedly.

Freddie quickly lied, "I'm okay. My legs are just hurting. I need to go to the bathroom."

Sharee started to push Freddie, but he stopped her. "No. You stay here. I got it."

After struggling to get into the bathroom, Freddie closed the door and then pulled a bottle of pills from his pocket. His hands trembled as he twisted the bottle open and tossed a couple of pills into his mouth.

A minute later, Freddie wheeled himself back into the living room with a forced smile on his face.

"Are you okay, Dear?" Sharee asked.

Freddie replied, "Yeah, I'm good."

Marcus bent down and secretly handed a small bag to Freddie. He whispered, "I got you something to help with the pain, man. Whatever you need, just call."

Freddie took a quick peek inside the bag, then nodded to Marcus.

Marcus patted Freddie on the shoulder and walked off to mingle with the crowd.

Hours later, the final guests shuffled out of the house. Marcus was the last one to leave, stopping at the door to grab Sharee's hands as he looked her in the eyes. "You know what to do. You got this."

Sharee nodded and Marcus turned to leave. "See ya later, Freddie, my man! Remember, I got you. We all do."

Sharee closed the door and walked toward Freddie, sitting down on the couch next to him nervously.

"Thank you," Freddie said.

Sharee asked, "For what?"

"For getting everyone together like that. It felt good."

Sharee didn't respond, instead looking down at the floor while fidgeting with her hands.

"Hey, what's up?" Freddie asked.

Sharee looked at him nervously, but didn't respond.

"What's on your mind, Ree? You can tell me."

"I was going to tell you a few days ago," she finally said, "but then with your injury..."

"What is it?"

"I just don't know what to do?"

"Please, Ree, just tell me."

Sharee sighed deeply, "I'm pregnant."

Freddie sat there in shock.

Sharee continued, "I know this isn't the best time, but we'll figure things out. I promise."

"I'm...I'm going to be a father?" Freddie finally murmured.

Sharee nodded.

"But, look at me, Sharee. I'm broken! How can I take care of a child when I can't even fucking walk?"

Sharee started crying and ran out of the room, leaving Freddie even more desperate and afraid. He pulled the bottle of pills from the bag and quickly threw a couple in his mouth, swallowing hard.

Chapter 35

As Freddie's thoughts returned to the present, he felt the pain in his knees return with a vengeance like an unwanted in-law. He opened the medicine cabinet and rifled through the bottles of pills there until he found the bottle of Vicodin. He popped four of them into his mouth and swallowed hard. *Now, that's the sign of a true pill-popper,* He thought, *when you don't even need a glass of water.*

As the drugs coursed through his veins, Freddie was assaulted by a barrage of memories from his past. He saw Sharee's face and felt a surge of guilt and remorse. She was the one he had wronged the most. She had been his rock and his angel, his only source of hope in his darkest hour. She stood by him faithfully, even after he pushed her away. Pregnant and devoted, she was there to comfort him when the pain became unbearable. And when Freddie talked about a comeback against all odds, she was there to offer encouragement only to follow that up with compassion when he finally succumbed to the reality that football would no longer be a part of his life.

However, as Freddie thought about it day after day, replayed the scene repeatedly in his mind, he slowly convinced himself that Marcus had meant to deliberately hurt him. He saw the fire in Marcus' eyes and the rage on his face as he charged toward Freddie. He had tried to cast that thought aside, nearly convincing himself that it was indeed just an accident. But the doubt still lingered in the corner of his mind, scratching there softly.

But losing football wasn't the only cause of his descent into the pits of human filth and degradation. The doctor had warned Freddie that any concerted effort to play again could put too much of a strain on his knees, and would likely lead to increased damage. He didn't listen and paid the price.

On the day that he 'officially' announced his retirement, it wasn't only his heart that was hurting. The nine months of strenuous workouts that he had gone through as soon as his post-operative therapy was complete had taken their toll, just as the doctor had warned. The inside of his knees had become so twisted and torn that a loud grinding noise emanated from them as he walked up the steps to the podium to speak.

The pain medication quickly became like candy to Freddie, as he started popping them into his mouth at every opportunity he had. When the effects of the prescription drugs became insufficient, he supplemented that with alcohol. It didn't take long for him to spiral out of control after that.

He quickly went from being a social drinker who hung out with friends occasionally to a nightly binge, often leaving him in a total stupor. And on those occasions when the pills and alcohol weren't enough, a quick line of cocaine did the trick.

Freddie covered up his drug addictions for quite a while,

hiding behind his more obvious drinking problem. However, one day Sharee walked in on him in the bathroom as he kneeled in front of the toilet, his blow lined up neatly on the toilet seat. Her face lost all color as she looked at the man who had once been her lover and best friend now reduced to nothing but a low-life junkie.

She slammed the door and walked out on him. "I am not raising our daughter in a drug-infested home!" she cried out as she left, carrying their daughter in her arms.

And so, Freddie finally lost the last two things that meant anything to him. He was now all alone.

A brief sigh issued from his lips as his thoughts returned to the present and he reached to close the medicine cabinet door. When he looked at himself in the mirror, the reflection rippled as if a stone had been thrown into a still pond. Freddie's eyes became empty sockets, glaring back at him from the glass with black blood oozing down the front of his face. He tried to open his mouth to scream, but a hoard of maggots squirmed from within, cutting off his voice. He tried to back away from the horror, but found that he was completely paralyzed.

The light started flickering again, and all Freddie could do was watch in terror as thousands of venomous insects and arachnids invaded the room. The sound of them scurrying and clacking across the tile floor was deafening. His skin tingled and spasmed as he felt them climbing and crawling all over his body. Panic shot like a rocket through his mind as he felt sharp fangs stabbing at his flesh. Powerless to act, he stood there motionless while the blood inside his veins boiled.

***

"I knew you'd show up, eventually."

Michael opened his eyes and saw that he was standing in the middle of a small apartment. Belial was sitting in a ripped-up black leather chair opposite him, one leg crossed over his other knee and his hands locked together on his lap. Off to the left, Michael saw a man standing paralyzed inside a small bathroom; being overrun by thousands of creatures. Blood oozed from his body, where sharp fangs had pierced his flesh. The man trembled under the attack, and he could almost hear him screaming silently.

Belial waved his hand, and the bathroom door slammed shut. "We need to have a little talk."

Suddenly, Belial was right behind Michael, "And it's me who's going to be doing the talking. You see, what we have here is a failure to communicate."

Belial paused and smiled, "I've always loved that line."

He bent down low and whispered into Michael's ear, "By now, you realize it doesn't matter who you are. That poor fool in there is the last one. Once he spills his own blood, just like the others, my victory is all but assured. And I'm damn sure not going to let a shit-stain like you fuck up my plan!"

Michael suddenly felt himself floating in the air. The bathroom door opened and his body flew quickly toward the helpless man until he felt himself merge with him. His own essence fused with Freddie's—every tissue, every fiber—until they became as one. Then Michael felt the poison sear through this own body—white-hot pain that engulfed him as his own blood boiled.

"Let's see how strong you really are, shit-stain."

Then Belial was gone.

As Michael stood there, unable to move, he watched in

horror as the face in the mirror—a reflection on the glass that wasn't his—began to melt. He listened helplessly as chunks of his flesh fell off and splattered onto the floor. Panic thundered into his brain and he knew this time he was going to die.

Chapter 36

As suddenly as the terror had started, it was gone. The blood disappeared from Freddie's face, and his normal eyes stared back at him from the mirror once more. He looked around and saw that all the creepy crawlies had vanished.

"What the fuck was that?" Freddie exclaimed as he fought to control of his nerves.

"You're finally losing it, Freddie, aren't you?" he said to his reflection. "The one last thing I can still claim as my own, my mind, is finally being taken from me, too."

A soft breath blew on his cheek, as a low husky voice whispered in his ear, "Oh, I assure you, you're quite sane, Freddie Smith."

As these words drifted into his mind, he saw Marcus materialize in the mirror behind him. "I have a secret I've been hiding for a long time." He smiled wide. "And I think you're gonna be really surprised."

A small voice squeaked out of Freddie, "What do you mean? What kind of secret?"

Marcus grinned wide and evil, "Your accident, the one that

ripped your life apart, wasn't an accident at all. It was planned. I had been looking for an opportunity. And when I saw that opportunity, I pounced on it—literally."

Freddie couldn't believe his ears. "No...it can't be. You were my best friend. You couldn't have done something like that."

"But haven't you blamed me all these years? In your mind, wasn't I the reason your life was ruined?"

It was true. Freddie had blamed Marcus, which was a normal reaction in an extreme situation. "I still loved you like a brother. How can you say you did that on purpose?"

A scene unfolded in the mirror. It was Sharee answering the front door, dressed in a bright red silk teddy. When she opened the door, a tall black man entered the house. Sharee pounced on the man, wrapping her legs around him as he held her by the waist. Their passion was an instant inferno that couldn't be extinguished.

Freddie's mouth dropped. He couldn't believe what he was seeing. Then the man turned so Freddie could see who it was. He gasped and staggered backward when he saw Marcus looking back at him.

"How could she?" Freddie murmured.

"How could she?" Marcus replied emphatically. "You were so wrapped up in yourself that you neglected everything about her that was beautiful."

Freddie's voice cracked as his eyes misted over, "But I gave her everything."

"You gave her nothing! You gave her things; worthless possessions that mean nothing to a woman searching for her purpose in life. Every time she turned to you, you shut her out, leaving her cold and empty."

"You're wrong," Freddie said softly. But in his soul, he felt a pang of guilt. Marcus had spoken the truth. He had given in to the temptation of fame and stardom and had forsaken everything he loved.

"Oh, and one more thing—have you seen your daughter lately? She's growing up to be quite a beautiful young lady. She has her father's eyes." Marcus' eyes flashed bright blue and a hideous laugh filled the room before the image faded away.

At first, Freddie didn't comprehend that last statement, but as he looked deeply into his own brown eyes, he understood. Now, the very last thing in this world that he had clung tightly to, his only real accomplishment, was no longer his.

He cried out and smashed the mirror with a fierce blow that bloodied his knuckles and sent fragments of glass flying in every direction. They reflected the light like tiny prisms as they cascaded to the floor with a tinkling sound, shattered like Freddie's soul.

A loud beep suddenly sounded on the TV, drawing Freddie's attention away from the disaster on the bathroom floor. He shuffled into the living room to see a commercial of a well-dressed man sitting at a news-anchor desk come on the screen. His voice was like an infomercial salesperson trying to get you to buy another kitchen gadget you didn't need. "Have you ever had the love of your life desert you in your greatest hour of need? Did you find out later that she cheated on you with your best friend? Were you ever in an accident that ruined your life forever? Have you finally reached the lowest depths of human suffering, with no light at the end of the tunnel?"

Freddie stood transfixed with his eyes open wide.

"If that describes you, Freddie, then there's only one thing left for you to do!"

The word suicide flashed onto the screen and scrolled across the bottom like a rolling banner with the latest stock quotes or news headlines. The salesperson continued, "That's right! When life has taken you down as far as you can go, and there's no hope in sight, then the only way out is for you to end it all! Take your life right now and be free from the pain and anguish that torments your soul. Do it now. Do it quickly. Then you can finally be free of your suffering."

A scoreboard suddenly filled the screen. The results: Marcus 69, Freddie 0.

The TV flickered for a second before another commercial came on, but Freddie barely heard the ad. He turned and shuffled back to the bathroom. He looked at the broken fragments of glass that remained on the medicine cabinet projecting a shattered reflection back at him. Then he took a deep breath to gather his nerve before he grabbed every bottle of medicine he had, limped back to the couch, and plopped down.

As he emptied the bottles one by one into his mouth, he thought of Sharee and the life he used to have. He thought of the girl he now knew wasn't his daughter, and he hoped she would grow up to be something special. He didn't think of football, though, and realized at the end, before his life flickered out, that it never should've mattered as much as it did. He had let life pass him by, and now he entered death full of regrets.

A minute later, Freddie started shaking violently and foaming at the mouth. Then he closed his eyes and went to sleep, never to wake up again.

Chapter 37

Michael's heart broke as he kneeled beside the couch where Freddie had just taken his own life.

"See, I told you it wouldn't do you any good," Belial said smugly.

This time, instead of reacting in fear, Michael looked at him defiantly, "This isn't over!"

Belial stood up, anger radiating from him like heat from the sun.

"You dare threaten me? Don't you realize who I am, boy? I was once a mighty general in Lucifer's army!"

"Yeah, and if I remember right, you lost."

Michael realized his mistake as soon as he spoke. The fury in Belial's eyes flared like a volcano, erupting with rage. He felt a jolt of pain as the fallen angel clenched his throat and lifted him into the air, choking him. "I think it's time to learn some respect, you little fuck!"

Belial reared back like a pitcher preparing to fire a fastball toward home plate and hurled Michael toward the far wall of the apartment.

Michael felt his bones shatter as he burst through the plaster and plummeted outside, landing face down on the pavement. A weak cry escaped his lips as he struggled to move. He felt a warm gush of blood spilling out around him onto the cement.

Belial walked over and crouched down beside Michael's broken body. "If you know what's good for you, you'll stay out of this," he said. "If not, I'll be forced to rip your scrawny ass apart, limb-from-limb."

As Belial turned and walked away, Michael heard Dr. Samuel's voice echo in his head, *Remember, he only has power over you if you let him.*

It was a sliver of calmness among the cyclone and Michael snatched onto it. He closed his eyes and focused. *This isn't real. It's all just a dream,* he thought repeatedly.

Slowly, he regained movement at his extremities and pushed himself off the ground. "Not so fast, you bastard!" he said defiantly.

Belial stopped and turned around. He glared at Michael for a second before he smiled and chuckled. "Okay, fine. Have it your way."

Suddenly, a barrage of metal flew up from the pavement—a combination of re-bar, electrical wire, and conduit. The wire snaked around Michael's arms and legs and yanked him backward so that the metal shafts impaled him all over his body—several through his arms and legs; three ruptured out of his stomach, with another two through his chest; and one that had entered at the base of his neck and extruded from his mouth. Blood gurgled out as he struggled to speak.

Then he went quiet.

***

Michael laid on the bed, his body twitching faster than before. His eyes darted back and forth frantically beneath his closed eyelids as his body writhed on the table.

"You need to do something, Doctor!" Mary pleaded desperately. "Please, wake him up!"

Dr. Samuel leaned over Michael, pulling his eyelids up to examine his pupils. The eyes seemed trapped in a state of terror.

Dr. Samuel replied, "If I pull him out now, it could cause irreparable damage, both physically and emotionally."

"But...you can't just leave him like that!"

Dr. Samuel pulled a needle from his jacket pocket and injected something into Michael's arm. A few seconds later, Michael's shaking calmed.

"What did you give him?" Mary asked.

"Just a little dose of Diazepam to calm him down."

Mary looked at him confused.

"Valium," Dr. Samuel said.

"Is it okay to wake him up now?"

Dr. Samuel shook his head. "Not yet. He needs to fight these demons on his own. It's the only way for him to become strong enough to fulfill his destiny.

"What do you mean by destiny?" Mary asked warily.

Dr. Samuel said quickly, hoping to cover up his Freudian slip, "I simply meant that he needs to be strong in order to live his life without fear."

Michael suddenly shot up in the bed and screamed loudly, before slamming back down unconscious.

***

Dr. Madison sat in a chair opposite the chaise lounge where Michael lay, with a pen in her hand and a notepad on her lap. She eyed him subjectively for a moment. "How are you feeling today, Michael?"

"Okay, I guess," Michael replied.

"Are you sleeping better?"

Michael just shrugged.

"What about the prescription I gave you? Has it helped?"

"Not really."

"So, you're still having nightmares?" Dr. Madison continued.

Michael answered simply, "Pretty much."

Dr. Madison jotted some notes in her pad and sighed. "I have an idea, Michael. If you're okay with it, I'd like to try a new approach."

Michael immediately grew skeptical. "Like what?" he asked.

"We need to get at the heart of these nightmares, so I'd like to try some regression therapy."

Michael eyed her suspiciously, "What's that?"

"It's a type of hypnosis that'll allow us to take your mind back to a younger time so we can try to get at the root cause of your episodes."

A wave of fear instantly crashed over Michael.

"It'll be okay, Michael," Dr. Madison reassured him. "Remember, it's all in your mind. Nothing can hurt you. I'll be here the whole time."

After a moment of hesitation, Michael nodded. "Just do what you gotta do, Doc. We need to fix this."

"Okay, good. Now I want you to close your eyes and take a deep, slow breath. Feel your whole body relax."

Michael closed his eyes and did his best to let himself go numb. After a couple of minutes, he felt more calmed than he had in a long time.

Dr. Madison continued, "Now, I'm going to count slowly backward from five. When I reach zero, you're going to feel yourself completely at ease and your mind open."

Michael settled deeper into the chair.

Once Dr. Madison had counted Michael down, she studied him closely for a moment before continuing. "How are you feeling, Michael?"

Michael was silent for a second, before he suddenly cried out, as the image of Julie standing on the ledge of the building flew into his brain. "I see...a woman. She's...desperate. She's crying on a ledge outside a tall building."

The scene shifted quickly to Harold sitting on the edge of his bed with the barrel of a gun in his mouth. "Now...it's man...with a gun. He's so sad. A picture...on the nightstand...his family. He's crying."

It switched to Jacob as he drove his car off the road into the raging river. "A man...in a tuxedo...crying. Alone. Wedding day. He's lost. He can't go on."

Then it was Freddie emptying countless pill bottles into his mouth. "A broken man...fallen from grace...no reason to live."

Tears streamed down Michael's face as Dr. Madison studied him for a moment. "It's okay, Michael," she said softly. "It's just your mind compartmentalizing the unwarranted guilt you're holding inside. Calm yourself, and think back further, to your childhood. Remember when the dreams first started."

Michael took a deep breath and calmed down. His eyes fluttered and his head rocked back and forth from side to side slightly as his mind searched his memories.

It settled on a young, ten-year-old Michael sitting in the backseat of a car looking excitedly out of the window as happy music played on the radio. His father was driving, while his mother rode in the passenger seat. His little brother, Dustin, was sitting next to him.

A smile spread over Michael's face. "I'm riding in the car with my parents. Dustin is in the backseat sitting next to me. It's my birthday. We're going out for pizza and ice cream."

Dr. Madison jotted down a line of notes in her notepad. "That sounds nice, Michael."

The scene continued with a steady rain covering the road ahead of them. "It's raining though. Pretty hard. Then the wind..."

The rain continued to pour, growing in intensity, as the wind howled across the road, reducing visibility to almost zero, and making it hard to keep the car under control. Suddenly, the vehicle hit a slick patch of wet pavement and started spinning. Michael's voice became agitated. "We're spinning...losing control...Dustin is crying...Mom Is screaming! It happened so fast!"

As the car spun helplessly into the oncoming lane, a truck blared its horn seconds before impact.

Everything went black for a moment, then the scene changed again. Michael was lying in a hospital bed with a sad-looking priest standing over him. "Suddenly, it stopped. Everything just stopped. When I wake up, I'm in the hospital."

Tears fell from Michael's eyes as his voice came in broken splinters. "I see a priest. He has funny marks on his hand. He tells me it's a miracle I'm alive. My parents and brother aren't. I can see it in his eyes."

Flash-forward, and Michael's parents are standing at the foot of the hospital bed, looking at him with warm smiles.

Behind them are several other people, strangers he has never seen before, all dressed in an array of garments from different places and different times. Each one walked forward and put their hands on Michael's forehead.

"I see my mom and dad standing at the end of my hospital bed. They're happy. And the room is filled with other people that I don't know. They're all smiling at me, like they know me, though. They're praying for me.

Michael's body quickly became more agitated, and he cried out again as he found himself immersed in a black void. A small crib in the center of the blackness was the only thing in existence. The only sound heard through the nothingness was a chorus of hissing. As he looked up from the center of the crib, a soft cry escaped his infant lips.

"I see myself as a baby...Everything around me is dark...There's something here, with me...Something evil."

Dr. Madison grew worried as she scribbled in her notepad once again. "Remember, you're safe here, Michael. Nothing can hurt you," she said unconvincingly.

The blackness slowly dissipated, replaced by a violent red and orange shifting light. The hissing clarified into the crackling and popping of a fire that had penetrated the void, snaking around the crib with its tentacles of flames.

Michael screamed in pain. "Everything's on fire...I Can't breathe...The smoke is choking me!"

The flames quickly engulfed the crib, and within seconds, Michael was on fire, his flesh melting from his bones. "The fire...it Burns!"

Dr. Madison jumped from her chair and rushed to Michael. "It's not real, Michael. It's only in your head."

She tried desperately to hold his shoulders down as his body shook violently. "I'm going to count back from three, Michael," she said quickly. "When I reach one, you'll come out of your hypnosis and return to the real world."

Michael thrashed about wildly, as the doctor struggled to subdue him.

"Three...feel yourself coming back to the present...two...the past is behind you now...one...you're safe now back on the couch in the office."

Nothing happened. Michael continued to flail about helplessly, crying out in pain. Desperately, Dr. Madison pleaded, "Come on Michael, come back to me. It's not real. It's all in your head."

Tears ran down Dr. Madison's face as she helplessly watched Michael wracked in pain. Then suddenly he stopped and grew still. She looked at him worriedly for a second, and reached forward.

After an agonizing moment, a gasp rushed from Michael's mouth and he sat up.

Dr. Madison looked at him questioningly. "Michael?"

Michael started coughing. "My throat feels like it's on fire."

"What do you remember?" Dr. Madison asked.

Michael was silent for a moment. He turned and looked at her through tortured eyes. "Everything."

He bent forward, and a gasp flew from his mouth when he saw a large burn mark on the back of his hand. He jumped to his feet as the fire ignited again, crying in terror as the flames wrapped around his arm, encircling him like a fiery anaconda. The stench of burning flesh filled the room as the blazing serpent grew quickly to encapsulate Michael completely, silencing his final scream.

***

Michael opened his eyes and looked around frantically. He

was still in Dr. Samuel's office, with Mary standing next to him. She had the same scared look on her face that he had grown accustomed to recently.

He yanked the sensors away from his scalp, causing the tape to rip his skin away in places. But Michael hardly felt it as he worked desperately to rid himself from the electronic web. Once he was free, he leaped from the table and ran for the door.

The doctor yelled out after him, "Wait, Michael, don't leave!"

But Michael had already swung the door open and was halfway through, running for an escape that had proved forever elusive.

Chapter 38

Belial took a deep breath, trying to calm his nerves, and walked down the long hallway. In all his time on this earth, he had never encountered a person who aggravated him as much as this one. He knew he shouldn't let the little man get under his skin, but he couldn't help it. He just kept coming back again and again, like a pesky mosquito. One he'd like to squash.

"Fucking little shit-stain!" he mumbled. "Who the hell does he think he is?"

Nazur joined him a minute later. "The subjects are ready for your inspection, my lord," he said in a haughty voice.

Belial cleared his thoughts. He needed to focus on the task at hand. He had a job to do; a world to crush; an apocalypse to start. If he succeeded, he'd finally get to go back home.

"Were there any problems?" Belial asked.

"Freddie was a bit of an issue, but we got him under control. He kept scrambling around with a crazed look in his eyes. We had to use a little bit of force to contain him. They're all ready."

"Thank you, Nazur. That'll be all for now."

"Actually, My Lord, I have some information that you might find interesting," Nazur said.

Belial raised an eyebrow. "And what might that be?"

"It seems the human you're interested in is more than just a lowly junkie. At first, it was difficult to trace his lineage since he was adopted as an infant, but after a little bit of digging, I found the Nun who oversaw the process and persuaded her to tell me everything she knew. It seems your 'shit-stain', as you like to call him, is a direct descendant of Joseph."

"You mean the Joseph? As in, Mary's dick-wad of a husband?"

"Yes, that's the one. Although, in this case, it was his second wife, Isabel."

A look of recognition flashed in Belial's eyes. "So, this is the offspring of the one that got away? The result of Cassius' failure?"

"It appears so," Nazur replied.

"That doesn't really mean anything. Everyone on this planet is a descendant of someone."

"One of my spies also indicated that Gabriel has been keeping a close eye on said 'shit-stain'."

Belial's eyes flashed red when he heard Gabriel's name. "Now, that changes things. I think it's time to turn the tables on our friends there. They won't be expecting us to know we're onto them. Whatever intervention they have planned for 'shit-stain' boy, we need to blow it up before they even get started."

Nazur replied, "And what do you have in mind, My Lord?"

Belial grew silent for a second, contemplating what his next move would be. "I can't afford to divide my attention right now, so I'll need to enlist the aid of someone with a very special skill-set to deal with this situation. Fill Nybbas in on everything you've found and let him do what he does best."

Nazur's eyes grew wide, "The Sandman? You want to release him? He won't be easy to catch again once this is complete."

"If he accomplishes his task, then I'll consider his sentence served. Besides, once the world has fallen, he can do whatever he wants. It won't matter."

"Very well, My Lord," Nazur said. "Consider it done."

With a renewed sense of purpose, Belial strode toward the first door on his left. He stopped and pulled the viewing window open. A smile played across his face when he saw Harold sitting on the edge of his bed with half of his face blown off.

Harold had been a lot of fun. It gave Belial a chance to do a little role-playing, something he was especially good at.

When he turned his head and saw Belial, Harold whimpered and tried to mouth something, only to expunge a flow of blood and mucus onto the floor.

Belial chuckled as he closed the window and walked across the hall to the next room.

Directly opposite Harold was Julie. She had been much easier to manipulate than Harold, given her fragile emotional state and feelings of insecurity. The result had even been a little more artistically dramatic. Plus, she had been the first, and everyone knows the first one is always the best.

He slid the little window on her door over and peeked inside. Julie was lying in the middle of the floor, her body twisted and broken at unnatural angles, trying desperately to move.

"Don't worry, dear," he said. "We'll have you fixed up soon. And I promise you'll be magnificent."

She replied with a pained murmur before Belial closed the window on her.

A short distance down the hall, Belial paused at the third door and opened the small window to peer in. This room held Jacob, who was sitting on his knees with a stream of water pouring from his mouth and ears. His skin was a dying shade of blue and his veins showed through like a giant spiderweb covering his body.

Belial couldn't resist and tapped on the glass to get Jacob's attention. "Here, fishy, fishy," he goaded.

Jacob turned toward him and a volley of water shot out that caused Belial to take a step backward as a puddle formed at the base of the door.

He closed the window and walked across the hall to the last door. When he looked inside, he saw Freddie scurrying around, swatting at a swarm of invisible insects. He stopped to scratch at his skin and pulled patches of flesh from his body.

"I can see where they might've had a little trouble with this one," he said.

Belial smiled as he closed the window and proceeded down the hall, whistling triumphantly. *They are perfect*, he thought.

Belial's plan was simple: first, he would unleash his beasts, whose destruction would be legendary; then, when the world was in ruins, his children would lead his army into the ultimate battle, all in the name of Lucifer. Then Belial would swoop in to save the day. It was the perfect scheme to clear his name and allow him to return home.

He pushed through the door at the end of the hall eagerly. The room beyond was a dark and dreary place, with mottled gray walls covered in mold, and tiled flooring littered with blood and urine stains. The smell of bile and excrement matched the décor of the room perfectly.

Tables and chairs were scattered haphazardly throughout the expanse, with no sense of conformity. Among these were seated his children. Broken and malformed each one, society had deemed them worthless, but for him, they would become an unstoppable force. These were the worst of the worst, and they were his.

Playing the evangelical once again, Belial held his arms out wide in welcome. "My children! How is everyone feeling today?"

A chorus of excited murmurs rose from the group. Belial looked around the room at his gathering beaming with pride.

From Dimitri Androve, also known as 'The Butcher of Main Street', who had slaughtered twenty-seven women and children, dicing them into bite-sized morsels he passed off as beef in his butcher shop, before skewering himself on his own meat hook as the police closed in on him; to sweet Mary Ingles, who had been kidnapped and raped repeatedly by six men over three months until she finally escaped, only to return two weeks later and put a bullet in each one's brain before turning the gun on herself. And there were many more with stories such as these, each one extraordinary in their own unique way.

Belial continued, "I hope you're ready to have some fun?"

Howls and cheers rose from the disfigured group.

A group of orderlies entered the room, each one wheeling a gurney with one of the four tortured souls strapped down tight upon it. Nazur directed the placement of the subjects, jotting down on his clipboard enthusiastically.

As the four captives struggled against their bindings, a young woman in a skimpy nurse's uniform strolled in, pushing a small cart with a silver tray on top. She stopped the cart near Belial before she turned back around.

"Thank you, Mercy," Belial said as he took a playful swat at her ass before she got out of reach.

A tiny squeal of delight escaped her lips before she walked out of the room.

Four large syringes filled with a silver, milky substance lay atop the tray, the mixture swirling inside the tubes as if alive. Belial walked to each bed and injected the liquid into each of the subjects arms. It only took seconds for their bodies to begin to shake and spasm as white foam gurgled from their mouths.

A hush engulfed the room.

"Now for the magic ingredient!" Belial said with a gleam in his eye as he grabbed a scalpel from the tray and sliced his wrist open. He proceeded to each table with his arm above the subject. The angelic blood slithered into their mouths like amoebas trying to escape the light. A black mist then enshrouded each one in a web of inky tentacles.

Lightning shot down through the ceiling, striking the center of the beds, sending the four individuals crashing to the ground. When the dust settled, a black orb hovered above each of their heads. The orbs moved in unison and shot forward, embedding themselves into their chests.

Agonizing wails erupted from the four as they writhed on the ground under the onslaught. Fire engulfed their bodies, filling the room with the smell of charred flesh.

The crowd watched expectantly.

When the fire dissipated a moment later, the four stood transformed to face Belial, each one regarding him with an icy coldness. They were pure evil standing before him.

Belial smiled wider than perhaps he had ever done before. *They are magnificent! There's no way I can lose now!*

He addressed the audience proudly, "My children, I give to you those who will usher in a new era and bring us to the promised land."

A chorus of cheers flew up as Belial surveyed each one.

Harold had grown to twice his size and was now a green-scaled behemoth. He held a giant battle-ax in his hands, which he swung with powerful might to shatter the floor at his feet. War was his name.

A giant serpent had taken over Julie's body. Her lower extremities were an enormous mass of glistening scales that coiled and writhed as she moved, while a portion of her female torso remained, giving her long arms that ended in sharp and deadly talons. Her cobra hood, now the hood of Pestilence, spread wide across her back in warning as her forked tongue darted in and out of her sharp fangs. A sharp hiss came from her mouth as she spat a stream of green venom toward the floor in front of her. The tile crackled and sputtered as the acid ate away at it, sending a cloud of toxic smoke into the air.

An eerie green glow surrounded Freddie's body as he stood there now as Famine. Both his mouth and eye sockets were dark voids filled with the same black nothingness that his soul had become. His flesh appeared as a giant living, moving mass, with insects scurrying around just under the surface. He opened his mouth wide and a swarm of locusts flew out.

Last, but certainly not least, was Jacob. A black mist swirled around his body. His flesh had disintegrated, leaving behind only his skeletal figure. He pointed his bony finger at a patient seated nearby, a young man named Wiley, one of the newer guests at Belial's asylum. Wiley responded with a look of surprise before his body exploded outward in a shower of blood and guts that would've made Gallagher proud. Death to all.

The crowd roared in approval.

Belial said, "I give you my Four Horsemen of the Apocalypse that will bring the world to its knees. Remember, it was Lucifer that deceived us all, and he needs to pay for that deceit. Now is the time for us to turn the tables and claim the paradise we deserve. Once Heaven realizes how wronged we were, they will have no choice but to let us in."

That last part was a lie. He knew that Heaven would have nothing to do with them. He was the only one that belonged there.

Belial reveled in the thought that he would finally be accepted by his brothers and sisters once again, free to roam the Emerald City, to dance upon its lush grass, to breathe in its sweet, everlasting fragrance. His plan had been successfully put in motion. The world would fall quickly, Lucifer would pay for his deceit, and Heaven would welcome him back with open arms.

A large smile spread across his face as each second brought him closer to his prize.

Soon, he thought. *Very soon.*

***

While Belial basked in the glory of his upcoming war and his plan to return to a world where he didn't belong anymore, Fierna quietly slipped from her hiding place at the back of the room, pulling the cloak tight around her to keep herself concealed. For a brief second, she had considered jumping up and exposing her dad for the fraud that he was. But she knew it wouldn't do any good. He had them all wrapped around his finger, ready to do his bidding no matter the cost. They were simply his marionettes, and he was the ultimate puppeteer.

Instead, she pushed her way through the throng of

outcasts gathered—those that he had sanctimoniously called his children—and quietly slipped through the rear door. Once she was clear, she threw the hood back and stormed down the hall muttering sharply to herself, her nostrils flaring and her hair aflame once more. "You're going to regret turning your back on me, Father!"

As she rounded a corner, eager to leave the confines of the asylum far behind, she collided with Mercy, who was walking in the opposite direction, knocking a tray from her arms that spilled a collection of vials onto the floor, each one containing a different color liquid.

"Fierna!" Mercy said as she crouched down to retrieve the elixirs. "I'm surprised to see you here. I know how much you despise this place."

"Don't worry," Fierna said. "I'm never setting foot in here again."

"Never is an awfully long time, especially in Hell."

Fierna scooped one of the vials from the floor as Mercy gathered the others, and looked at it closely. The liquid inside was a bright red with veins of silver swirling through. "What is this for?" she asked curiously.

Mercy looked at her nervously. "I can't tell you. The boss will have my hide—literally—if I do."

The flames from Fierna's hair hissed as she slammed Mercy against the wall. She whipped a dagger from her belt and held it against Mercy's throat. "Answer the question, bitch, or my father's anger will be the least of your troubles."

"Okay," Mercy pleaded. "Don't get crazy here. The potions are for the ones locked up in the high-security wing. Apparently, they're supposed to augment their powers somehow. I think he's creating some sort of a backup plan in case his horsemen fail."

Fierna was shocked. "So, he's not convinced his plan will

succeed?"

"Hey, I just work here, but to me, it's more like he's just throwing as much shit at the wall as he can and hoping some of it will stick."

Fierna withdrew her knife from Mercy's throat and walked away. "Thank you, Mercy. You've given me an idea. I know just who I need to find to help me put an end to my father's madness."

"When this is over, come back and see me some time," Mercy called out.

Fierna barely heard her as a plan began to form in her mind, one that would finally teach her father a lesson.

The end

Book Two Preview

Coming Soon

Hellish

Book Two:

The Chosen

By Scott Dokey

Chapter 1

The Himalayas.

For ages, they have ignited the imagination of countless legends and devotees. The most glorious of them was the Dhankar Monastery. Crowned like a royal fortress on the highest cliff of the Spiti Valley, it watched over the Spiti River that glittered and roared far below. The monastery had concealed its ancient mysteries and miracles, uncorrupted by modern society. This was its greatest power. Its inhabitants tasted a bliss and peace that few could comprehend. Only the fearless and daring braved to scale the harsh and dangerous mountain slope to reach it. But once they did, they were met by a blaze of light and music that overwhelmed them with awe and ecstasy that made them never want to leave.

But a hidden world of mystery and power lay under the earth's surface unknown to the human world. In the dark depths of the underground, a huge cavern shone with a faint light. The walls of the colossal cavern were inscribed with ancient symbols of power, forged by the hands of forgotten masters. They formed a barrier of arcane force that repelled any unwelcome visitors. In the heart of the chamber, a luminous pool shimmered with mysterious light. The Archangel Michael gazed into its depths with a troubled expression on his face. Flanking him were his fellow archangels: Gabriel on his right and Azrael on his left.

"It's time to reveal everything," he said. "His soul is struggling right now and we are running out of time."

He turned toward Gabriel. "Go quickly. Show him everything. In the meantime, Azrael and I shall prepare the army for battle."

***

He found Michael huddled on a park bench, staring blankly into a small pond before him. Even though the weather outside was balmy, Michael was scrunched up close to himself, his knees pulled up to his chest on the edge of the bench, and shivering visibly. His eyes bore the sadness of a thousand tortured souls in them.

"Michael Davis?" Gabriel asked.

Slowly, Michael turned his head and thought for a moment that he must be dreaming again, caught up in another maddening nightmare that would soon turn into a dark struggle for his sanity.

Gabriel sat down next to him. "Don't be afraid. I'm not here to harm you," he said. "I'm here to help."

"How can you possibly help?" Michael asked. "I don't even know you?"

"But I know you. And I also know that the nightmares are over. They won't bother you again."

Michael was shocked. "How do you know about that?"

"I know everything, Michael, and I've been sent here to help. My name is Gabriel, and I'm one of the Archangels."

"Now I know I'm fucking crazy!" Michael laughed.

Gabriel remained calm, "Look into my eyes and you'll see that I speak the truth."

Michael turned his head and was instantly spellbound. Perfection radiated in those eyes. A wave of tears engulfed him as he felt the totality of his own imperfections, recalling each moment he had slipped into darkness, too weak to fight his own personal demons.

Gabriel touched his shoulder gently, and he felt a soothing warmth flow through him.

Michael looked up at Gabriel. "Why is this happening to me?"

Gabriel was thoughtful for a minute before he spoke. "It's all quite simple in its reason. It's the never-ending struggle of good versus evil. Only this time, Belial has come up with a plan so diabolical, so ingenious in its manufacture, that he may succeed."

Michael didn't know what to make of the stranger sitting next to him. "Who is this dick, Belial, and why does he keep trying to kill me?"

Gabriel chuckled. "Belial is one of the fallen angels that served Lucifer and was cast out when he was defeated. He was his first in command and feels like he was wrongly expelled from Heaven. Now, he's trying to weasel his way back in."

Michael was stunned as he tried to wrap his head around what he'd just heard. "But what does any of that have to do with me?"

Gabriel looked at him for a moment, measuring Michael's countenance. "Ages ago, we put in place a weapon that we may use against evil if the situation ever called for it. You are that weapon, Michael."

Michael's jaw dropped as the words echoed through his brain, assaulting him as if someone had rung a huge gong only inches from his ears, and his mind once again became a swirling merry-go-round of confusion.

"What the fuck did you just say?" he asked, barely able to get the words out of his mouth.

"Try to calm yourself, Michael," Gabriel said. "I have something I want to show you."

The Archangel vanished for a brief second, only to reappear with a stack of newspapers on his lap. "For you to understand, I must start from the beginning."

He handed the papers to Michael. "Look at these and tell me what you see."

Michael's heart stopped as he saw Harold's face on the cover of the Indianapolis Star. The headline shouted: 'Man takes his own life after family perishes in a gruesome accident'. He devoured the article and realized that it was a mirror of his haunting dream. He tried to push away the images of the man's agony, but they clung to his soul like leeches.

He saw the dead women on the bed as Harold tried to escape the nightmare, their devilish eyes smirking at Michael as they sprang to life in an otherworldly display. He watched sadly as Harold was sentenced to death for crimes he hadn't committed, then heard the slice of the guillotine as it sped downward. Then 'Reverend' was torturing Harold until he had no strength left to fight. Finally, he saw Harold kill himself again.

Michael's face lost all color by the time he finished the article. He turned toward Gabriel, tears falling down his cheeks as he spoke. "I saw him in my dream. It was so clear that I felt like I was there."

"That was a vision you were seeing, Michael. It was not merely a dream, but the future about to happen. The images you saw were very real indeed."

A million questions circled inside of Michael's brain like a horde of vultures waiting to descend upon a dying animal lying on the desert floor. Not one of them issued from his lips, though. Instead, he picked up the next newspaper and started reading.

This one was the Chicago Tribune with the headline: 'Woman leaps to her death after a day of treachery'.

Michael's heart crumbled when he saw Julie's picture radiating happiness on the page. He remembered the sting of failure when she was fired from her job, followed by the blaze of anger and hatred when she witnessed her husband's betrayal and deceit. He recalled the flash when Julie teetered on the narrow ledge, haunted by the shame of her sins. Then he watched her body explode onto the concrete far below. And once again, Belial's image came flying into his brain.

Taking a deep breath before proceeding, Michael picked up the next one. It was the Washington Post this time: 'Wedding day ends in horror after Bride leaves Groom at the altar'.

He had beheld the most splendid day of a man's life turn into a hell of torment. He knew from his own anguish that nothing crushes a man's heart like losing his love. It can rob him of his honor, hurl him into insanity, and annihilate all his sense of self. Here, a man snuffed out his own life because of it. He felt the water choking his lungs again as the monster's jaw clamped onto his leg, while Belial gazed on with cruel eyes.

He placed the paper on top of the other two at his side, leaving Freddy Smith smiling up at him from the L. A. Times on his lap. Beneath his picture was the heading: 'Former NFL star dies of a drug overdose in his downtown apartment'.

Michael had admired Freddy's talent since his college days. Indeed, the whole world had expected Freddy to be a legend for generations to come. Then the unimaginable happened, leaving the sports world in disbelief and Freddie's life shattered. His fall from grace was swift and complete, leaving him with no way to climb back up. Finally, he had ended his struggle and surrendered to the darkness surrounding him. Then Belial's words rang through Michel's brain, *'You're too late. He's the last one.'*

Slowly, Michael put the paper down on top of the others and looked at Gabriel sadly, wiping the tears from his eyes with the sleeve of his shirt. "These people all went through so much shit until, in they all believed that suicide was their only way out. And I felt every second of it."

"You feel that way because you are a compassionate man. In that regard, you are truly a blessed soul. But also know that in these cases Belial had a direct hand in their outcome."

"Yeah, and he also tortured the fuck out of me while he was at it!"

"Your pain is temporary, Michael. I assure you; you will grow to be much more than you are today."

Michael scoffed. "What does that even mean?"

Instead of answering his question, Gabriel continued, "As I stated before, Belial is convinced that Lucifer tricked everyone into following him into battle, knowing that they couldn't win. At first, his anger consumed him and he went on a rampage, searching for evidence to support his claim. Since then, he has grown desperate to return home. We learned of his plan while observing those four individuals as they being born. Terrible complications developed during each birth, and in a couple of the cases, the mother died. Belial had cursed the souls of these children while still in the womb."

"But why these four?" Michael asked.

"Are you familiar with the book of Revelations?"

Michael felt embarrassed. Here he was, a junkie sitting on a park bench talking to an angel about the Bible, shameful that his ass hadn't touched a church pew as far back as he could remember. "I know a little," he admitted sheepishly, "from when I was younger. Are you talking about the Apocalypse?"

"That's precisely what I mean. However, the book of Revelations points to the fact that the Horsemen are instruments of God. Belial plans to create his own Horsemen that he may use toward his end. As they sow the seeds of death and destruction on the world, he plans to blame the whole thing on Lucifer, and upon defeating Lucifer, he will present himself to our Father as the obedient son he thinks he is. Then the gates will be open to him once more."

Michael was stunned. "Can he win?"

"Possibly. As soon as we realized Belial's plan, we took steps to prepare for his 'manufactured' Apocalypse. In the same way that he doomed those four souls to use for his wicked purpose, we chose four individuals to become weapons against the evil."

Gabriel urged Michael to turn toward the pond, "Look into the center of the water and I'll show you."

As Michael leaned forward and peered deeply into the water, a small ripple began, starting from the center and working its way outward. Then a series of bubbles rose to the surface from deep below, releasing a foul stench into the air.

A black, inky tentacle suddenly shot out and wrapped around Michael's chest, pinning his arms to his side, and dragged him into the water before Gabriel could react. A final bubble broke the surface of the water before everything went still.

Michael was gone.

Author Bio

Growing up in the shadow of Notre Dame's Golden Dome, Scott Dokey developed a strong affinity for the arts, learning at a young age the joy of transforming an empty page into something magical. Eventually, as an adult, his creative endeavors expanded to include writing and filmmaking. Focusing primarily on subjects with horror and supernatural aspects, he became an award-winning screenwriter, and has produced and directed three short films and a no-budget feature film.

Scott currently lives in Southern California with his wife, Jennifer, and their daughter, Kaylee, enjoying the sweltering 120° summer heat. Of course, 85° in January more than makes up for it.

To find out more about his work visit his website at www.scottdokey.com

www.ingramcontent.com/pod-product-compliance
Lightning Source LLC
Chambersburg PA
CBHW020401120726
47904CB00002B/655